THE GIORDANA CONNECTION

A Scott Stiletto Thriller 6

BRIAN DRAKE

WOLFPACK
PUBLISHING
— EST 2013 —

WOLFPACK PUBLISHING
— EST 2013 —

Paperback Edition
Copyright © 2019 Brian Drake

Published in the United States by Wolfpack Publishing, Las Vegas

Wolfpack Publishing
6032 Wheat Penny Avenue
Las Vegas, NV 89122

wolfpackpublishing.com

Paperback ISBN 978-1-64119-657-4
eBook ISBN 978-1-64119-656-7

Library of Congress Number: 2019951413

THE GIORDANA CONNECTION

Author's Note:

My sincere apologies to the wonderful people of Twin Falls, Idaho, for the way I depict your town. It's such a nice place that I couldn't resist using it for this story. Unfortunately, dramatic license requires that I mangle it a little. Let's call it an alternative-universe Twin Falls, and not reflective of the real thing.

Brian Drake
San Francisco, CA
2019

CHAPTER ONE

Twin Falls, Idaho

Stiletto missed the last cab. There had been four when the bus pulled into the station. By the time the luggage had been removed from the compartment underneath the vehicle, of which his bag was one of the last, the cabs had picked up fares and driven away.

Stiletto stood under the roof of the outer pickup area, taking in the night sky and deserted parking lot. The brightly lit area of the Greyhound station made the parking lot seem much darker than it really was.

The bus had entered Twin Falls, Idaho via Highway 93, Scott's first introduction to the city at night being a darkened apartment complex and a well-lit Target parking lot.

Stiletto turned his head and noticed a woman standing to his right. She approached him nervously. She wore a long coat that wasn't buttoned up, leaving a waitress uniform partially exposed. "Did you see a girl on the bus? About twenty-five, red hair?"

She folded her arms and shivered a little. She was about as tall as Scott, maybe in her early forties, with her blonde hair tied back.

Stiletto said, "I'm sorry, no." There had been plenty of girls on the bus, but none had matched the description. Stiletto had cataloged each person during the journey, watching their comings and goings at the various rest stops. It was a hard habit to break even though he was among civilians, not in a war zone. He was back home in the United States, where presumably the Russians with their still-open contract couldn't find him, but the survival instinct was ever-present. It wasn't all bad, because when watching for thorns one seemed to notice the roses, but the readiness to launch into a fight made settling down tough. The Russians might indeed reach him in his homeland. They'd certainly shown a willingness to assassinate others the Kremlin deemed enemies on American soil.

He knew that all too well, and he couldn't take any chances. He knew the Russians had the power to wipe him out, and with his disavowed status with the Central Intelligence Agency, there would be no penalties for the Kremlin.

He watched the woman's reaction. Her body seemed to sink under an invisible weight. "Thank you," she said, then turned and began walking toward the parking lot. Out there alone, she would make the perfect mugging victim.

Or worse. Stiletto glanced around but saw no potential threats.

"Hey," he said. "I missed the cabs. Any chance you could give me a ride to my hotel?"

She stopped and turned slowly. Her sad eyes watched him for a moment. He wondered what she thought of him. He wore no jacket, just a long-sleeved black shirt, wrinkled, with the sleeves rolled up. Forearm muscles bulged. He'd been on the road for almost forty-eight hours and felt gross. He probably looked less than presentable as well.

She might take him for the threat he was watching for, he realized. She might have told him there were three very decent hotels across the street. Stiletto, of course, saw the signs, but he wasn't staying at any of those.

"I'm staying at the Hyatt downtown," he told her. "Shouldn't be too far from here, right? I'll pay you."

The woman took a deep breath. "I'm sorry. I...uh... "

"It's okay."

"But, yeah, the Hyatt isn't far. A few blocks."

She pointed in that direction, but Stiletto didn't ask for specifics.

"I can walk, that's fine," Scott said.

He wanted to sound jovial, but his voice shook. Sure, he could walk. There was nothing wrong with his legs, and he had the GPS capability of his smartphone should he wander in the wrong direction. That didn't bother him.

Walking alone bothered him. He didn't know what

was waiting for him in the shadows. He felt like an alien in his own country. He was a man on the run, from himself and others, and that made him want to run faster. But here he was, stuck at a bus station with butterflies in his stomach. He'd faced down an untold number of enemies in his career, but none of those encounters had scared him like the idea of walking in the dark did now.

The woman smiled good-bye and crossed the parking lot to slide behind the wheel of an old Honda. She turned right out of the parking lot, and the engine whined as she picked up speed.

Stiletto plugged the Hyatt's address into his smartphone's GPS and started walking, the verbal directions set to a low volume. He dropped the phone into his shirt pocket and slung his heavy tote bag across his back and chest. It was full of a few days' worth of clothes, a shaving kit, and his Colt .45 auto pistol. He started for the sidewalk and walked on the hard concrete. His shoes tapped loudly, almost too loudly. The noise would give away his position to anybody waiting in ambush. The few streetlamps created more shadows than light. All the buildings on either side of the street were dark, mostly likely offices open only during the day. That explained why the street was so quiet, too. He was alone and his heart started to race. He felt like a man who had awoken to discover he'd been buried alive. He quickened his pace. The lights of downtown lay ahead, seemingly miles away. The shadows of the trees and bushes gave him a start.

Anything could be hiding there.

Too many battles. Too much violence. You're not a kid anymore. You've lived with violence for so long you can't relax.

Whose fault was that?

Mine?

Theirs?

Was there a way out of his rat's maze?

The Honda had stopped half a block ahead and sat idling at the curb. Wrong side of the street, but it didn't matter. There was nobody else around. Stiletto walked by without looking. The driver's window whispered down. "Hey."

Stiletto turned. The glow of the dash turned the woman's face green.

"Get in."

The passenger door opened easily and Stiletto dropped into the seat, jamming the tote between his knees. She drove off and made a right at the next light, merging with the heavy boulevard traffic. Stiletto turned off the navigation on his phone, let out a sigh, and relaxed his tense shoulders. It felt good to be in a busy area. It felt good to be in a moving vehicle that provided at least some protection.

The woman said nothing and they rode in silence for a while. He felt like he should start a conversation.

"Who were you waiting for?"

The woman took a moment before answering. "My

daughter."

"Shouldn't we go back and see if she's on the next bus?"

"You were on the last bus." Her hands tightened on the wheel. "I was there for the three buses that came before yours, too."

"Can you call her?"

"Why do you care?"

Stiletto shifted in his seat. "Maybe I shouldn't be asking."

"I'm sorry. I don't mean to be rude."

"It's okay."

"My daughter's name is Monica. She told me she wanted to come home and get clean, but she wasn't on the bus."

"Shouldn't you call the police?"

"And tell them what?"

"That your daughter is missing."

The woman brushed back her hair. "I don't know where she's missing from. Well, other than here, her home, but that was a long time ago."

"You didn't send her the bus fare?"

"She told me she'd saved the money. All she wanted was for me to be at the bus station when she got here."

"Didn't she tell you where she was coming from?" Stiletto said.

"I haven't seen or heard from Monica in almost three years. I was just glad to finally hear her voice."

Stiletto said nothing more. He knew all too well the pain of knowing somebody was close but also out of reach. For him, two people were out of reach forever.

Maddie, his dead wife.

And Felicia, the daughter who wasn't talking to him. He'd give anything to be in the woman's position. At least her daughter was trying to communicate.

The situation made his gut hurt. He looked out the window at the passing scenery and hoped the woman didn't detect what he was feeling.

CHAPTER TWO

She stopped for a light. "My goodness," she said, "I haven't told you my name and you know part of my life story."

"I'm Scott."

"I'm Chloe. What are you in Twin Falls for?"

"Nothing special. Just passing through."

"On your way to somewhere else?"

"I guess so."

"You don't seem too sure."

"That's all I know for now."

"Oh, I'm—"

"It's all right, don't worry. Now we both know parts of each other's life stories."

She drove forward again and they passed the next three blocks in silence. The sign for the Hyatt glowed red in the distance, most of the tan-colored building highlighted by the ambient lighting scattered throughout the property. Chloe turned her car into the full parking lot and pulled up at the front. She fished a business card out of her worn leather purse. "Here. I run a diner. Come by tomorrow. My treat. Don't worry about paying for the ride."

Stiletto took the card. "I'll come by for breakfast. Thank you."

He climbed out of the car and watched her drive away. After checking in, Stiletto went up to his room. He unzipped the tote bag, set out shirts, jeans, the shaving kit and underwear on the bed. The last item out of the bag was a hard metal case, gray and battered from years of use. A safe sat next to the television stand. Stiletto knelt in front of it and punched in the combination the hotel had posted on its door. He set the case inside and followed the instructions for how to set his own combination. He chose a five-digit number that spelled out "Delta." He had never spent a day in Delta Force, instead serving with the Green Berets during his Army career, but he liked the name as a safe code.

From room service, he ordered a plate of chicken strips, salad, and a Coke. The operator told him it would be about forty-five minutes since it was past midnight, but Stiletto didn't mind. He sat in a reclining chair near the bed, which was aimed at the television. He flipped through TV stations, finally settling on a Hogan's Heroes rerun, where the enemy was foolish and the solutions to problems were easy to achieve.

When his food arrived, he turned the television off—Sergeant Schultz was in the middle of claiming once again to know nothing—and ate, but he couldn't stop thinking about a missing daughter and the mother who wanted her home. She was out there somewhere.

Chloe needed help.

Help he should provide.

Because he could. He had talents and abilities that weren't meant to be hidden under a bushel. He had a responsibility to help others who lacked a champion. It was a blessing. And a curse.

Stiletto ignored the thought and ate quietly, enjoying the light spice in the crunchy breading of the chicken strips. The salad was well-prepared, with croutons and bacon bits, as ordered.

He thought about Chloe. He hadn't told her the truth about why he was in town. It really wasn't any of her business, and he didn't expect she'd be involved in any way. He was in Twin Falls to do a favor for a man he had met on his last mission in Venezuela, a CIA agent named Tim Pierce, who also had a daughter.

Heavily beaten by a dictator's thugs, wounded, and in bad shape, Pierce had doubted his survival despite Stiletto's attempts at keeping up his spirits. After he had broken the CIA man out of a Venezuelan prison and taken him to refuge at a Catholic church that doubled as a hospital, Pierce had asked Stiletto for a favor.

"I got a kid. Daughter. She lives in Idaho. Twin Falls. If anything happens to me, you know—"

Stiletto froze. He knew all too well what Tim Pierce was asking, and there was no way he could say no.

"I'll do whatever you ask, Tim."

Tim Pierce opened a pocket of his prison jumpsuit. "I kept this from the prison guards," he said, handing Stiletto a folded photograph. Stiletto took the picture. "Her name is Shelly."

The photo showed a pretty blonde woman in her 20s. She had green eyes, and a smile that, Stiletto assumed, resembled her mother's, but she had her father's nose. Fathers and daughters were connected like that.

"Tell her, you know, her old man—"

"I get it. I have a daughter too."

"Yeah."

The two men said nothing for a moment.

"You better get going. Win the war, rock star."

Stiletto, aiding Venezuelan rebels in a violent coup against their oppressors, had indeed brought the war to a close. Pierce had not survived, and now Stiletto had to follow through on his promise. But what did you say to the daughter of a man who had died protecting others?

"Your father died in battle, but he wanted me to tell you good-bye and that he loved you very much."

It was something. It was the truth, anyway, but nothing else that came to mind seemed good enough. He'd taken the bus into Twin Falls instead of a plane to buy time; time to think about what to say to the young woman when he found her, and time to consider what he would do once he finished the job.

There was never any doubt in his mind that he'd find

her. It was the kind of job Stiletto couldn't refuse.

The day might come when he had to ask somebody for the same favor.

CHAPTER THREE

The morning wake-up call jerked Stiletto from sleep. His pulse beat rapidly as he leaned over to pick up the handset. He had sweated a lot during the night and felt the warm moisture all over his body.

"Yes?" He sounded breathless.

A robotic voice told him this was his requested wake-up call.

Stiletto hung up. His watch said 7:45. Sunlight wanted to blast into the room, but the still-closed drapes held it back. Stiletto regarded the drapes for a moment.

There's no danger here. No snipers across the street.

He felt better with the drapes closed, though. Because there might be snipers across the street.

The prospect of a hot morning shower to bring a fresh start to the day pulled him out of bed. He turned the spigots and set the stream to warm, stepped in, and let the spray hit his body while he unwrapped the small bar of soap all hotels provided, wondering for the umpteenth time why the soap had to be so small. Couldn't they spring for a larger bar? Better yet, couldn't Stiletto remember to buy his own? The United States was still a free country. That meant Scott didn't have to use inferior soap products if he didn't want to.

Give me decent soap, or give me death!

He laughed. If bad jokes could shake him from his funk, he'd buy a book of bad jokes and read it from front to back until he felt better.

He took his time in the shower, and shaved slowly as well, making a mental note while dressing to see if the hotel had a guest laundry room. Or maybe he could send his clothes out. After spending a few minutes studying a city map, wishing he was playing tourist so he could spend time hiking outside the city, he set out for a long walk. A cab would have been nice, but he wanted to see the city up close. He doubted being so exposed was the right choice, but he forced himself to go forward.

He had to admit that his life's work was wearing down on him, and it was something he didn't want to admit, because it meant he wasn't invincible. He was coming to terms, he realized, with his own mortality. The pressure of the Russian threat, as well as the constant state of combat in which he found himself, were taking a toll.

There would be a breaking point, somewhere along the way, if he didn't find a means of defeating the external and internal threats.

Downtown was crowded, with chain stores and more cars than pedestrians. The steady stream of people kept

Stiletto alert and jumpy. He stopped to look at something or changed his pace whenever another pedestrian stepped too close. While browsing a magazine rack in a corner grocery store, he told himself all this would pass. He would eventually open the drapes in his room. Deep down, he wasn't so sure. He was a man with a target on his back. He couldn't drop his security for a moment.

He picked up a couple of H. Upmann Nicaraguan and Davidoff cigars at a liquor shop, the terrific blend by AJ Fernandez, along with a lighter. The lighter was a Zippo with an 82nd Airborne Screaming Eagle on one side. He hadn't served in that unit, but he had served in a similar one, so what the hell. He lit the cigar and kept walking. The smoke helped keep people away, and he ignored the dirty looks from some who didn't like clouds of smoke in their face. It helped identify friend and foe, he decided. An enemy wouldn't care about the smoke if his job was to get close enough to put a bullet in Stiletto's head or a knife in his ribs.

He reached Chloe's diner and took cover in an alley across the street. He finished the cigar and watched the surroundings for any danger signs.

Prior to him accepting the mission in Venezuela from Number One, the leader of a group of retired intelligence professionals known as The Trust, the old man had said he might be able to get the Russians to back off if he became a full-time operative for the group.

Stiletto hadn't given the man an answer, promising

instead to think it over. The more he considered the idea, the smarter it seemed.

Since being fired from the CIA for the unauthorized mission to Russia that put the price on his head, he'd been working as a freelance contractor, taking the jobs he wanted and keeping his eyes open for other situations where people needed somebody with his skill set.

Life had not been easy since he had been let go from the agency he'd called home for so long.

And it wasn't getting any easier with time.

He'd have to have a long talk with Number One and discuss the details, but Stiletto decided joining The Trust was in his best interests. He needed help. He couldn't continue on his own any longer. What had seemed like a Sir Galahad crusade after getting booted from the Agency was now putting him in serious jeopardy, and not only physically. The mental threats were worse. It was time to rejoin an organization that allowed him the ability to do work that came naturally as well as offered him protection from outside forces.

But first, Twin Falls.

Through the front windows, Chloe's diner seemed busy. Full booths, counter lined with customers. The outer shell had been chromed in the style of '50s diners, with a rotating neon sign extending from the roof that announced Chloe's for all to see.

Stiletto stood in the smelly alley and finished the cigar. Customers entered and exited. His stomach told him to quit being an idiot. He tossed the cigar butt on the ground, waited for a break in traffic, and crossed the street.

The grill sizzled, the stocky cook standing by with a spatula, watching a pile of hash browns and two slices of ham. His belly bulged against his white uniform top. The booths weren't full anymore, and Stiletto spotted the two cops in one booth immediately. They were to his right. Both wore sharp black patrol uniforms with gleaming gold badges. The older of the two had a rough face, pock-marked and wrinkled, gray hair slicked back. Stiletto only saw the back of the younger officer's head. He knew he had to be younger because of his jet-black crewcut. Stiletto pivoted left and found a seat at the far end of the counter.

The low voices and sizzling food made the place odd-ly comforting. A young woman with pale skin and oily black hair came over and placed a glass of ice water in front of him. She asked if Stiletto wanted the morning special or a menu.

"What's the special?"

"Sausage and ham omelet, with the house salsa mixed by Chloe herself."

"Sounds good. I'll take that and hot green tea if you have it."

"Okay."

"Is Chloe here this morning?"

"Boss is always here."

"Tell her Scott is reporting as ordered."

The young waitress cracked a smile. As she went away, Stiletto knew the gossip machine would start cranking. They'd want to know who he was, why Chloe had invited him, and if they were going out. Stiletto glanced to the right as he sipped his water. The cook turned back to the grill. Stiletto smiled. Yup, the gears were turning. Then he saw the older cop staring at him and stopped smiling.

Chloe emerged from a back room a few minutes later.

"Enjoying the morning?" She leaned a hip on the counter.

"Exploring a little," he said. It was good to see her again. She had curly blonde hair, something he hadn't noticed the previous night. When she smiled, the space between her teeth showed. Stiletto found that attractive too. She added that his omelet would be on the house, as promised, and made sure the pale-skinned waitress knew that when she brought Stiletto his plate. More fuel for the gossip machine.

Stiletto wondered if Chloe had done that on purpose.

CHAPTER FOUR

Stiletto was nearly finished with his omelet when the two cops rose from their booth. The older officer went to the register, where the pale-skinned waitress asked the sergeant if he had enjoyed his "usual," and wouldn't he like to try something else next time? The cop let out a low laugh and said the usual always hit the spot. Stiletto faced forward as he ate but felt the cop's eyes on him. The lawman's attention was like a heat-seeking missile, and Scott was out of countermeasures. Stiletto swallowed another bite and wondered why he had blipped on the cop's radar.

The older cop presently came to the stool next to Stiletto. He picked his front teeth with a fingernail. Cleared his throat. The rumble in his neck sounded like thunder. Stiletto turned to the big man and smiled.

"Good morning, Officer."

"You like that omelet?"

The diner seemed to hold its breath. Only the grill made any noise, but the sizzle seemed muted.

"It's good. I like the salsa that's mixed in."

"Chloe does that sauce herself, you know. Her own private recipe. Won't tell a soul how she puts it together."

"Good for her," Stiletto said.

Stiletto looked at the cop's name tag. BOSKOWICTZ. He carried what looked like a Colt Python, a large .357 Magnum revolver, a handgun that Stiletto hadn't seen in a long time. Old-school hardware meant old-school cop, and Stiletto bet he kept a blackjack in his back pocket to go with the revolver. He wasn't in the same shape as when he'd first put on the uniform, though. The man had a noticeable paunch that his bulletproof vest didn't entirely conceal.

"Twin Falls is a peaceful city."

"I'm sure you do an excellent job of keeping it that way, Sergeant."

The cop's eyes narrowed. "I know your type. Keep it in your pants, hear?"

"I'm just trying to eat my breakfast, Sergeant."

Chloe yelled from the kitchen doorway. "Is there a problem, Carl?"

The cop kept his eyes on Stiletto but raised his voice in reply. "Just saying hello."

"You've said hello long enough, Carl. If you've paid your bill, please leave."

The cop tipped his head back and said, "You heard me," to Stiletto, then nodded good-bye to Chloe. He let the front door swing wide as he hit the street. His partner followed like a little dog.

Stiletto sipped his tea and swallowed another bite.

Chloe came over. "Okay?"

"What's the story with him?"

"He and my…uh, family, go back a few years."

"He thinks I'm some sort of suitor or something?"

She laughed. It sounded like wind chimes. "That's a word I haven't heard in a long time."

"I'm a bit old-fashioned."

"Who knows what Carl is thinking half the time? What are your plans for the rest of the day?"

Stiletto shrugged. "Whatever."

Chloe smiled, but the look in her eyes made her seem far away. She was still thinking about her lost little girl. "Let me know how that goes. Excuse me." She turned and headed back into the kitchen. Stiletto finished and left the pale-skinned waitress a tip equal to the omelet's cost.

Stiletto glanced at the picture of Pierce's daughter and the address jotted on the back of the photo, then looked up the location on his phone. She lived on the east side of Twin Falls, a quiet couple of blocks of warehouses and canneries sharing space with apartment buildings.

This time he did take a cab but told the driver not to wait. He walked around the block, trying to tell himself he wasn't doing a recon, but of course, he was. Trees lined the sidewalks on a block dominated by red brick buildings with only signs on the front entryways to tell them apart.

After the circuit, he stopped in front of the Chesterfield Apartments.

Nice tiled floor in the lobby and a desk for a receptionist, currently empty. A podium with a printed directory of tenants stood before the desk. He scanned the list for Apartment 406 but Shelly's name wasn't listed as the tenant. A man's name was.

Skipping the elevator, he climbed the stairwell to the fourth floor, his breathing just a little heavy as he stepped out into the hallway. Down the hall to 406. He knocked with nervous tension in his belly. Did Shelly no longer live at this address, or did she live with the man listed in the directory? A man indeed opened the door. He was sleepy-eyed and still dressed in his pajamas, with a robe loosely belted around his narrow waist. He looked at Stiletto and snorted.

"You're not holding a pizza," the man said.

"No, sorry," Stiletto replied. "I'm looking for somebody named Shelly Pierce. Does she live here?"

"I live alone, dude," the man said. "Your girlfriend might have been here before me, but I have no idea."

"She's not a girlfriend. I served with her father overseas, and I'm supposed to give her a message. Her old man didn't make it."

"I'm sorry. I'm not much help to you."

"How long have you lived here?"

"Maybe six months?"

"Thanks. I didn't mean to disturb you."

Stiletto wasn't sure what else to say. The man said he

had to get back to his show and started to shut the door. Stiletto didn't stop him.

He went back down the stairs, and his mind regrouped a little. Back in the lobby, the receptionist's desk still empty, so he tried a hallway that led to the manager's office. The manager sat behind a desk that was very clean except for the necessities, which right now included a stack of folders. He had loosened the collar of his shirt and his tie hung askew. The manager had the broad shoulders of a football player. He looked at Stiletto for a moment as if waiting for him to talk. Stiletto couldn't get his mouth to work.

The manager said, "Are you my ten o'clock?"

"No, actually," Stiletto finally said and repeated his story.

"I can't talk about previous tenants," the manager said. He offered his apologies, and Stiletto saw another person, a woman, approaching from the end of the hall. The ten o'clock. Stiletto muttered his thanks and retreated to the street. Outside, he stood on the corner and stared blankly into space. After a few minutes, he gathered his wits. Okay, she wasn't at the apartment. That meant she lived somewhere else. Maybe, worst case, he'd have to call his handler in Paris, Suzi Weber, and have her do a trace.

The trail wasn't cold. He kept repeating that as he started walking again. He would find her. He'd have to put in more time and more legwork, but he'd find her. He could not fail the man who had trusted him. Stiletto kept walking.

CHAPTER FIVE

Stiletto continued his exploration of the city as he thought his options over. Suzi, his handler in Paris who worked as a go-between for Stiletto with potential clients, would give him merry hell about another "freebie job" that neither received a check for, especially her. But he knew that if he asked, she'd drop whatever she was doing and look into the Shelly Pierce matter for him.

Locally, he might try the police, but he couldn't exactly call Shelly a missing person. A private investigator could also run a trace, which seemed like a good enough option until Stiletto realized he only had her name and a previous address, no personal information, such as a social security number. All he truly had was a name and a picture. A private eye would need more.

Heck, Suzi would need more information, too.

The sidewalk crowd had thinned out, but vehicle traffic seemed the same. The streets were narrow, one or two lanes in either direction, and there were too many cars, so everybody jammed up as a matter of routine. There were cabs and buses aplenty, and Stiletto decided to take advantage of one or the other when he became tired of hoofing it.

The tall buildings blocked out the sun, and on some blocks, the cool shade chilled Stiletto. He felt much better when he found the sun again. There were no mountains in view, only clear blue sky that seemed to lay siege to the city. The color was richer than Stiletto remembered from other cities in the United States.

He stopped at another alley, this one with no odor and what seemed like enough space for two cars to pass, and leaned against the wall. He faced the street and lit the second H. Upmann Nicaraguan.

He watched people pass until his eyes drifted to a billboard on the side of the building across the street. The cigar slipped from his lips, hit his shoe, and rolled onto the concrete, trailing smoke.

White letters on a red background.

A young woman's picture appeared on the left side.

DO YOU KNOW WHO MURDERED ME? DO YOU KNOW WHO I AM?

The girl had sandy blonde hair, cut short. She might have been anybody, but she wasn't anybody. She was somebody. She was Shelly Pierce. Stiletto recognized her nose. She had her father's nose. Stiletto's knees shook as he read the rest of the billboard.

ANYONE WITH INFORMATION ABOUT THIS WOMAN'S IDENTITY, PLEASE CONTACT "JUSTICE FOR JANE" OR THE POLICE. SHE NEEDS HER NAME BACK AND HER KILLER BROUGHT TO JUSTICE.

Stiletto stood staring, mentally paralyzed as a chill colder than the shaded streets rushed from head to toe. He didn't need to look at the picture in his pocket. He knew.

Oh, God, it's Shelly.

I'm sorry, Pierce.

I didn't make it in time.

Then the yellow taxi stopped at the curb, two men in blue business suits climbing out. They paid no attention to Stiletto as he slid into the back and told the driver to take him to the nearest public library. The driver, who chewed a toothpick and wore a bandana around his neck, hit the meter button and pulled into the street.

Scott Stiletto found a silver-haired woman at the reference desk. She asked if she could help him and Stiletto only blinked, trying to talk. Then he spotted a smaller cardboard stand-up of the billboard he had seen. He pointed to it. "This girl. I want to read about this girl."

A couple of bucks paid for a photocopy of an article from City Living Magazine. Stiletto sat on the cold concrete steps in front of the tall library building and read. Then he rolled up the pages and grabbed another cab. He told the driver: "Lakeview Cemetery."

The pale gray headstone read JANE DOE.

Below that, the date of her murder—six months earlier. He knelt before the headstone and traced a fingertip through the letters of the name. This was the one thing he hadn't prepared for. That he hadn't even considered. Who would?

Six months ago.

He let out a breath. At least she hadn't died while he was taking his sweet time flying to the US from Venezuela and then stalling for more time by hopping a bus to Twin Falls.

Stiletto pulled the folded magazine article from his back pocket. He slowly read it again, unconsciously moving his lips as he did. Jane Doe had had no ID on her body when police found her stuffed in a large duffel bag in an alley behind a restaurant. They had published a composite sketch of her face, but nobody had come forward with information. A $50,000 reward had brought in no useful leads and remained unclaimed.

Months had passed, the article said. The case had gone cold. Finally, a group calling itself Justice for Jane had put up the cost to bury her properly. The group had vowed that they wouldn't stop until they brought her killer to justice.

He tore a page from the article in half and grabbed from a pocket the cheap ballpoint pen he'd swiped from a library desk. He scribbled on the paper HER NAME WAS SHELLY, then went in search of a rock, but found a fallen tree branch instead. He weighed the paper down with the branch on top of the headstone and stepped back.

He'd found Shelly, yeah.

Now it was time to find her killer.

Stiletto owed her and her father that much.

He turned and walked away. He didn't feel like an alien any longer. Uncertainty had been replaced by determination.

Stiletto let his mind process the discovery while he walked, and presently, he found himself downtown. He stopped at a wide plaza with a fountain in the center. He moved through it slowly while everybody else seemed to move at high speed.

He found an empty bus stop and sat down on the cold metal bench. The sun had begun to set, and with that came a cold chill. With no tall buildings or mountains to block the wind or the setting sun, the brilliant orange was a sight to behold, but Stiletto barely noticed.

He stared straight ahead, unmoving, unaware of the

activity around him. A bus pulled up to the stop, its engine loud and its exhaust pungent, but Stiletto only stared through it. If the driver even wondered if the man on the bench would get aboard, he didn't wonder for long, since he put the bus in gear and rejoined the flow of traffic.

He moved his head, looking down at the hands resting on his lap. It was one thing to have a mission. It was something else to figure out how to accomplish the mission. The answers would come with time. He wasn't going anywhere.

Then he looked to the left. The neon CHLOE'S sign blazed up the block. He left the bench and started toward it. No hiding in the alley this time; he pushed open the door and saw Chloe behind the counter. She was scratching something on an order pad. She looked up and smiled, then the smile faded. Stiletto moved slowly to the counter.

Chloe touched his hand. He looked at her. Chloe said, "What's wrong?"

Stiletto finally unloaded his story on her. She listened quietly. He didn't get a chance to finish before the cook called out an order. Chloe excused herself. She told him she was covering for somebody who was sick, and she'd be back ASAP. Stiletto sat still while life continued around him.

CHAPTER SIX

Stiletto didn't touch the tea she brought. He made circles on the table with the mug, watching the liquid. Chloe sat across from him. They'd moved to a corner booth in the back. A few customers remained.

Stiletto told her about his work as a military contractor, leaving out his background as a CIA agent who had been fired for disobeying orders and wound up with a price on his head put there by the Kremlin for reasons he no longer felt comfortable thinking about. He was in Twin Falls to keep a promise to somebody who had died during his last mission. He told her about the billboard, his library visit, and leaving the note on Shelly's headstone. Chloe let him get the words out without interruption. Once he'd fallen silent, she finally spoke.

"I paid for the headstone, Scott."

He frowned.

"I joined the group almost as soon as it formed," she said. "That girl reminded me of Monica. All I could think about was my own baby out there somewhere, so I joined and wrote the check for the headstone."

"I need to see the guy who wrote that article."

"He's part of the group, too. Let me call him for you. I know he'll want to talk to you, and he can probably tell you more than I can. I didn't spend much time at the meetings, so I missed a lot."

"Why?"

She waved a hand, shook her head. "Long story. My father thought it was a bad idea to get involved. He and I don't get along, and it was typical of him. But you don't want to hear my history. Let me call Billy for you, okay?"

Chloe gave his hand another squeeze and slid out of the booth. Stiletto didn't watch her go. He stared into the tea. Dipped the tip of a finger in it. The tea had gone cold.

Chloe shut the door to her small office in the back of the diner. She sat down hard in the chair behind her desk and put a hand to her heart. It was beating fast, her pulse racing. Who was this Scott fellow? Was he the person they'd been waiting for, the one who might provide the answers they wanted?

Her hand trembled as she picked up the telephone receiver and dialed a memorized number.

"City Living Magazine."

"Billy Cooper, please."

"One moment."

Chloe waited. She noticed a bruise on her right thigh above the knee. She probably bashed it on the edge of a table and didn't remember. Her uniform skirt covered it while she was standing. She'd banged it against the side of a counter the other night while rushing food out to a customer.

"Billy Cooper."

"It's Chloe."

"What's new?"

She started telling the reporter about Scott in such a rush that he had to ask her to slow down and start over.

When she finished, he said nothing for a moment.

"You still there?" she said.

"Yeah. Wow. What a break this might be."

"I thought so too."

"When does he want to meet?"

"As soon as possible."

"Let's do it tomorrow." He gave her a time and place, a park where they could talk privately.

"We'll be there."

"Don't let this guy get away, Chloe."

"I won't."

They said good-bye, and she hung up. Sitting back, Chloe let out a breath, as if she'd been holding it underwater.

Chloe Giordana had been brought up in plenty, but adulthood had been a struggle because she refused any connection to her old life. Especially her father, now that her mother was gone. She didn't want his money. She didn't want him around at all.

The biggest lesson her father had taught her growing up was that nobody was going to give her anything. She had to earn it. Respect, status, money, whatever, and after seeing all the businessmen her father knew, she decided her own business was the way to go.

But what kind? She worked as a waitress through college and decided she would open her own restaurant, so she switched her undeclared major to business. When Jimmy Chiles, the fellow who had owned the diner prior to her, decided to retire, she borrowed money to take over the lease. She'd put her own name on the marquee because she didn't want to survive on Jimmy's coattails. That had been her first major business decision. Taking his name down from the marquee had been tough, but an action Jimmy supported because he knew what she was trying to do.

Her second big business decision was to not be invisible in the diner. She could have stayed in the back office during business hours, but she didn't. She put on a uniform and took orders with the rest of the crew because she wasn't above doing grunt work.

Refusing start-up money from her father had been another big decision, one that had been easy to make because she knew it would leave her beholden to him and his "friends." Around that time, she was already getting the idea that they weren't the kind of people one wanted to associate with.

Her father's business affairs had always been a mystery, her questions dodged with the assurance that they had plenty of money and she'd always have what she needed, but she'd watched enough gangster movies to start getting ideas. Some of her father's "friends" resembled the people Pacino and Liotta portrayed. They seemed to go out of their way to imitate those characters, with the big cars, the entourage of scary goons, and the assurance that they had nothing to fear from the law. What she witnessed had given her crazy thoughts, ones that wouldn't leave her mind.

After her mother died, she had confronted her father with a simple question.

"Are you in the Mafia?"

And just like that, as if he'd been caught in a lie and finally decided to tell the truth, her father admitted he was the big boss of the local syndicate.

CHAPTER SEVEN

Stiletto dressed the next morning, mentally preparing himself for the meeting Chloe had arranged with Billy Cooper, the journalist who had written the magazine article still crinkled in the pocket of his jeans. He opened the safe and took out the battered gray case, which he placed the case on the corner desk. The drapes remained closed, but the sliver of light that slipped between the fabric created a slice through the table and the case. Stiletto snapped the locks and lifted the lid. Inside was a .45-caliber Colt Combat Government Series 70, rebuilt and customized to his specifications. The automatic lay snug in a leather holster, but Stiletto quickly shut the case and returned it to the safe.

It wasn't gun time yet.

But soon.

"I'm glad you want to help," Bill Cooper said, "but what can you do?"

"Dammit, Billy—"

"Chloe, have I told you how many cranks we've gotten in this case? I wouldn't be here if you hadn't called."

"Funny, you didn't say anything like that on the phone."

"I have a right to ask the question, Chloe."

Stiletto watched the reporter from the other side of the table. They'd chosen a park for their meeting. The sun felt good on Stiletto's neck. Cooper wore wraparound sunglasses to shield his eyes. Cooper's wrinkled button-down shirt and wrinkled khakis matched his long curly hair, which grew wildly and resembled a bush.

The City Living writer kept his eyes on Stiletto through the dark sunglasses. The reporter's face was still as he waited for an answer. Scott felt like he was staring at a robot.

Stiletto said, "I can do things you can't."

"Like what?"

"Things the law can't or won't do."

"You're here playing the hero?"

"I'm not a hero."

Cooper waited.

Stiletto asked, "Did Chloe give you the basics of my story?"

"Yes."

"What did you leave out of the article?"

"Huh?"

"I don't believe for a second things happened the way you say they did."

"It's all there in my piece."

"The cops had nothing? Nobody came forward? No way."

"This isn't a large city. There were only so many—"

"It's not a large city, Mr. Cooper. There are more secrets in a small city than a large one. Trust me."

Cooper's face didn't move. The wrap-around shades were fixed on Stiletto. The wind ruffled the reporter's curls.

Stiletto continued, "Are you sure it's all there? What kind of town is this, Billy?"

Cooper blinked.

"Is there a syndicate that runs the show? Some political machine that calls the shots?"

Chloe said, "It's not like that here."

Her voice shook. There was no truth whatsoever in her words.

"You wouldn't know," Stiletto said.

"Hey—"

"Billy?" Stiletto said.

"Little bit of both," the reporter said. "Low-key."

"Always is."

Cooper nodded.

"Either the cops are lousy," Stiletto continued, "or somebody wanted Shelly's murder covered up. Why would somebody want that?"

"I don't know."

"Know any of the cops who worked the case?"

"The lead detective helped us out a little."

"I'd like to talk to your detective friend."

"And I'd like to introduce you. Her name's Erin Keene."

Stiletto nodded.

Stiletto started to light a cigar when Chloe said, "Not in the car," a little too sharply.

They rode in silence, Chloe's hands tight on the wheel. The Honda shook and rattled as the tires hit a rough patch of road.

Stiletto said, "I didn't mean to—"

"Forget it."

"I'm serious."

"I said forget it," Chloe said.

"All this reminds me… I mean, I'm just—"

"Scott, I understand. But I know more about what goes on around here than you think."

"What does that mean?"

"I told you to forget it."

Stiletto faced forward and said nothing more. It wasn't the time to press her, but her remarks reminded him that he really didn't know anything about her history. She hadn't volunteered much. He thought of the cop who had hassled him in the diner and her response to him. It was more than familiar. It was antagonistic.

There was a lot Chloe wasn't telling him.

He needed to find out what she was hiding.

Chloe dropped Scott at his hotel and headed home to her apartment.

She'd been fortunate that the diner had been a success from day one. Jimmy's endorsement had certainly helped, but eventually, he'd left Twin Falls for retirement in Florida. It had been a sad day when he departed. Chloe had felt alone for the first time in a long time, which had forced her to focus more solidly than ever on work.

She had her husband and a new baby, of course, so she wasn't totally alone, but Jimmy had provided a different type of support system. Now she had to fend for herself.

Chloe Giordana and Bruce Milosevitch had been high school sweethearts and had married after graduation from college. Monica had arrived a year later.

They'd balanced work and home together. Bruce was a good handyman who'd brought the diner up to the specifications Chloe desired and helped run the place. But then Bruce had run off with one of her employees, a much younger girl fresh out of high school.

He'd left a note saying good-bye.

Chloe was left to raise Monica and run the business on her own.

She'd made her father promise not to track Bruce

down and have him killed. Her father had promised he wouldn't. The fact that they'd had the conversation the way other people talked about sweeping the floor amazed her for all the wrong reasons.

Monica had been a tough girl to raise. She'd challenged her mother at every opportunity, especially when she reached the teenage years, but Chloe had managed to keep her fed and clothed and alive and run her diner at the same time. The effort had provided many sleepless nights and a lot of stress.

Monica fell into the wrong crowd in high school, discovering drugs and alcohol, addictions she couldn't shake. Now she was a runaway. She was an adult, able to make her own choices, but running away had been an odd one. Chloe didn't know why she had taken off. Some people were unable to stay away from drugs and alcohol; she understood that. She also knew those people could get help if they wanted it.

What made her run away? Monica knew all about her grandfather, so was that the reason? Chloe had no idea, and she suffered more sleepless nights and more stress, trying to search for the answers.

Presently she arrived home and stopped cold at her door. It was open about an inch.

For most people coming home to a sight such as an open door, it meant chills, fright, a dash next door to call the police.

But this was normal for Chloe.

It meant her father was inside.

She dropped her keys back into her purse and pushed it open. She turned the lock and set her purse in the kitchen. Fresh coffee wafted from the pot at the end of the counter. She turned into the living room, hands on hips, and frowned at the man standing by the living room window, blowing into the steaming coffee mug he held near his lips.

The man was tall and slim and wore a custom-tailored gray suit, a white shirt, and a black tie. His gray jacket was draped over one arm of the couch. He'd combed back his black hair, which needed a trim since his hair was starting to inch over the top of his ears.

Chloe said, "Comfortable, Dad?"

He didn't turn from the window. "Do you have to park on the street like that? It can't be safe at night."

He turned to face her. "Isn't there a garage under this building?"

Chloe crossed her arms, eyes narrowed, lips pressed together.

"You look good, sweetie," her father said.

She laughed. Her uniform was stained, and her skin was covered with a coating of long-dried sweat. She wanted to tell her father no, she looked hideous and needed a shower, but she kept her mouth shut. Why interact with him more than required?

She returned to the kitchen, grabbed the coffee pot from the machine, and poured the coffee into the sink.

"I just made that."

Chloe put the empty pot back in the maker, replaced the filter, scooped fresh grounds into the top, filled it with water, and hit the switch. She leaned back against the counter with her arms folded, her chest moving in and out with her rapid breathing.

"Chloe—"

"What do you want, Dad?"

"Tell me who your new boyfriend is."

"You gotta be kidding me."

"Carl told me about him."

"You know what I think of Carl Boskowictz."

"He says you gave the guy a free breakfast."

"You need to get out of here. Right now."

"Chloe—"

"Scott is not a threat."

Her father straightened a little, and Chloe wished she could push the words back into the mouth. A hot flush raced through her body.

Her father stepped closer. He was two inches taller than her. She felt his shadow and shrank a little. "Why would I think he's a threat? Why would you say he's not a threat?"

She kept her eyes on him. "Leave. Now."

Chloe's father took another sip of coffee, then placed the mug on the counter. The coffee machine burbled and dripped. The man grabbed his suit coat. He passed his daughter on his way to the door. "You've given me something else to think about, sweetie. Have a good night."

Chloe's father pulled the door shut quietly behind him.

CHAPTER EIGHT

"Carl?"

"This isn't a good time," Carl Boskowicz said.

Ben Giordana, Chloe's father, tightened his grip on the limousine's telephone. The big car shook as the driver sped up an on-ramp to join freeway traffic.

"It's never a good time, is it, Carl? You're spending more and more time with your other friend lately."

A moment of silence. Giordana listened to the rumbling road noise.

Boskowicz's voice went down a bit. "What do you need, Ben?"

Chloe's father smiled. He switched the phone from one ear to the other. "My daughter's friend. I'm going to need a little more information about him."

"Right. Okay."

"First thing tomorrow."

"I'll put some men on it."

"I want you to do it personally, Carl. Understand?"

Boskowictz cleared his throat. "I'll do it myself."

Chloe's father allowed himself a wry smile. "Thank you. I'm glad I can count on you."

Giordana ended the call and set the phone on the seat beside him. His lips formed a straight line, and his breathing was slow and steady. He made a tight fist with his right hand.

He and Chloe had been very close once, when he could hide his work from her. It had been easy. He'd been able to hide it from the police and FBI for two decades.

But as the top man of the Twin Falls "Outfit" his luck finally ran out when Chloe became an adult. That was when the strain began. That was when she put two and two together and came up with Mafia. He wanted to scream because a bunch of palookas on his payroll had tipped her off by pretending they were Al Pacino. Stupid gangster movies. They took all the secrecy out of the Organization, thanks to the "insiders" who were bitten by the Hollywood bug and had to spill everything they knew.

As long as her mother had been alive, they'd made an effort, but when Tammy died, Chloe had started pulling away, and a girl named Shelly Pierce had made his life worse.

Shelly Pierce was a secret he'd been able to hide from Chloe, which was critical since she insisted on helping those do-gooders on the "Justice for Jane" team. She had pulled away for good when he'd insisted she stay away from them. He'd sent Carl to keep the pressure on and to keep her from getting anywhere near the truth. He'd long ago forgotten if he was trying to protect her from what had happened or hide his culpability.

Who was the new man? Giordana needed a name. Carl had sensed trouble, and that kind of warning was good enough. The new man was trouble indeed.

If Chloe's new squeeze became the threat that she claimed he wasn't, Giordana would have him buried with all the other bodies the top man in the Outfit had been forced to have planted deep in the ground. He had a lot to hide. His closet was overflowing with skeletons. An outsider poking his nose in was a one-way ticket to a pile of trouble he might never climb out from under.

But his mind turned back to Chloe. No matter what, fathers loved their daughters. He and his wife Tammy had not been able to have another child, so Chloe was the only one. He figured the best way to get back in her good graces, to bring back the little girl he once knew, was to find her missing little girl. The situation with Monica had hurt his daughter deeply; she wore the pain on her face. Locating his runaway granddaughter was proving difficult, but he had men searching the country. They'd find her.

Giordana took a deep breath and shifted in the seat. He tried to relax for the rest of the ride home.

He had to admit, there had been no true relaxation for quite some time.

Stiletto grabbed a cab in front of the hotel. The driver whistled a tuneless tune as he drove Stiletto across town. Downtown, the streets narrowed, creating a long back-up. The buildings showed their age here. Brownstones mixed with sooty brick, bland and unattractive after so many decades.

O'TOOLE'S sat scrunched between a vacant building and a small hotel. The cab double-parked while Stiletto paid and told the driver to keep the change.

Two older men without jackets and smoking cigarettes braved the afternoon heat in front of the door. They stepped aside as Stiletto approached, but their eyes didn't leave him.

Despite the bright sun outside which fought to get in through the small pebble-glass windows, the bar was very dimly lit. There was oak paneling on the walls and quiet murmurs of conversation. Stiletto stood for a moment and let his eyes adjust. The bulky bartender watched him. The handful of customers, most in plainclothes with two or three in cop uniforms, glanced his way. He wasn't one of them, and they knew it.

"Stiletto!"

Stiletto looked left. Billy Cooper, the curly-haired reporter, waved from a booth. He again resembled an un-made bed, with an appearance that would have been more acceptable in 1968. Stiletto wanted to tell Billy Cooper it wasn't 1968 anymore.

A woman sat with Cooper. She had short hair, sported

no makeup, and wore a jean jacket over street clothes. She looked tired. Stiletto scooted into the booth next to the reporter.

Cooper said, "This is Detective Sergeant Erin Keene."

Stiletto extended a hand across the table. "Scott."

The short-haired woman shook the offered hand and leaned forward with her elbows on the table. "Billy's told me a lot about you."

"This is a cop bar," Stiletto stated.

"Yes."

"Can we step outside?"

"This place is private, don't worry."

"I need some air." Stiletto pushed out of the booth. The reporter and Erin Keene hurriedly followed and joined Stiletto on the sidewalk.

Cooper said, "Stiletto—"

"I don't trust the ears in there."

"It's okay, Billy," Erin said. "Why don't you excuse us a bit? Stiletto and I are going to take a walk."

The curly-haired reporter nodded and fished a crumpled pack of cigarettes out from under the left sleeve of his shirt.

Erin turned and started walking, Stiletto beside her. She was shorter than him but walked with a quick step. Her eyes might have looked tired, but Scott noticed she took in all the street details around them. He bet very little missed her scan.

"It wasn't our fault. There were four of us working

Shelly's case," she began. "Around the clock. She had a boyfriend we knew about. He vanished soon after Shelly's body was found."

Erin took another deep breath.

"She worked as a waitress at a diner. Two of her coworkers came forward—Penny and Vicki were their names—but then they stopped talking to us."

"Why?"

"Death threats."

"Of course."

"I wasn't going to risk anybody's life since I recognized what was going on. Call it a hunch. We focused on finding Chad, the boyfriend. I had his last name, Mendoza, so the apartment he and Shelly had shared was easy to find, but Chad never turned up. Completely vanished. We kept his name out of the press because we didn't want nuts showing up claiming to be him."

They reached the end of the block and turned left at the corner. The street inclined slightly.

"We expanded the investigation," Erin continued, "to see if maybe Chad Mendoza was involved in anything illegal. He had money but no known source of income. We thought maybe Shelly had seen or heard something she shouldn't have."

"Stop," Stiletto said. They stood for a moment. Both were a little winded from hiking the incline. "You thought Shelly might have been involved in something illegal too?"

The detective's eyes stayed on Stiletto's face.

"That's right," she replied.

"I would have thought the same thing," Stiletto agreed. He started walking again, Erin catching up.

Stiletto sniffed. "What happened with Chad?"

"We couldn't find anything to connect the boyfriend with a crime."

"That's it?"

"That's my story. Shelly's case went cold after that. The witness intimidation was the only thing we had to work with, and Shelly's friends refused to talk. Something more was going on, but I didn't want to risk my people or the witnesses. I figured we'd bust eventually somebody who could roll over on who did it and why. Sometimes that's the only hope you have."

Stiletto stopped, put his hands on his hips, and stared at a cluster of skyscrapers in the distance.

He told her what had brought him to Twin Falls without talking too much about Venezuela or his presence there. She was getting enough of that story on the news. But he figured she needed to know about Tim Pierce and his request, and why Stiletto was fulfilling it.

"I want to know who killed that girl," he said. "What's the chance of seeing the evidence you collected?"

"Zero."

Stiletto blinked.

"I appreciate what you're doing," Erin assured him. "Best I can do is set you up with her friends. There's no law stopping you from talking to people."

"If her friends wouldn't talk to you—"

"It's the only thing I can offer you."

Stiletto watched her. Her eyes remained on him as well. She had an agenda. If what he'd told the reporter was enough to get a meeting with the lead detective on the case and for her to offer him information on witnesses, he had a feeling he knew exactly what her agenda was. She was a hammer without a nail, and Stiletto was the nail.

Who was the board?

He said, "I appreciate any help you can provide."

Erin nodded. "I could use a corned beef sandwich. Let's go find Billy, and I'll spring."

Stiletto nodded and followed Erin back to the cop bar.

CHAPTER NINE

The quiet jazz on the coffee shop's speakers had recycled to the beginning of the CD by the time Penny Warren arrived.

Stiletto, sitting in a corner with his back to the wall, waved the tall redhead over.

"Hi," she said.

"Call me Scott," he told her as they shook hands. He helped her remove a long black coat, which she draped, along with her purse, over an extra chair.

They sat. Stiletto asked, "Where's Vicki?"

"She called and said she'd be a little late," Penny replied.

"I'm surprised either of you could make it."

"Detective Keene assured us everything was okay. She even offered to be here, but her word was good enough for me. I convinced Vicki, so here we are."

They faced each other, silent. She had blue eyes, and she blinked a few times as she examined Stiletto.

"So, you think you can do something?"

"I'm going to try."

A stocky blonde woman reached the table. "Hi, sorry I'm late." Penny rose and hugged the other girl. Stiletto stood and shook her hand.

"I'm Vicki," she said. They sat. Stiletto offered to buy a round of lattes, but both women declined.

"Detective Keene said you wanted to know what Shelly was doing before she died," Penny began.

Stiletto's jaw tightened. "Right."

Penny fidgeted in her chair. Vicki examined a thumbnail.

"Shelly and me and Vicki waited tables at Sugar Lanes," Penny said. "It was a bowling center with a little diner, always busy."

Stiletto nodded.

"Well, her boyfriend Chad was a regular," Penny continued. "Sometimes she worked late, and he liked to come by and see her. Sometimes he'd have a bunch of friends with him. Always the same four guys."

Vicki said, "Same creepy guys."

"Shelly couldn't stand them."

"Why?" Stiletto asked.

"Not sure," Penny said. "She always got really quiet when they were all together. I even heard her tell Chad once that she didn't want them around."

"What did they look like?"

"Big guys," Vicki said. "Can't really remember them

all." To Penny, "Can you? Anyway, there was one guy I do remember. He really made Shelly nervous."

"Damien, right?" Penny asked. Vicki nodded.

Stiletto raised an eyebrow.

"His name was Damien," Penny said. "I don't, I mean, I never knew his last name. Tall, bulky guy."

"Real black hair, like oil," Vicki added.

"None of us liked him," Penny continued. "It's not like we really knew him, but just having him around gave us a really bad feeling. Shelly felt even worse around him."

The two women fell silent. Stiletto said, "So that's it?"

"Well," Penny said, breathing deep, "eventually they all stopped coming around. About a week before Shelly… was murdered. That was also when she got really quiet, not talking to us much. She started making mistakes at work. Rookie stuff that she shouldn't have had a problem with."

Penny looked down at the table. Vicki said, "A day or two before she died, Shelly gave me her diary and told me to keep it safe. I have." She reached into her purse, removed a small key, and placed it before Stiletto. He stared at it.

"It's in a safe deposit box. Not even Detective Keene has seen it."

Stiletto rolled the key between two fingers as the girls' story circled through his mind. He tried to picture Shelly in her last days, but he couldn't get his mind around the image.

Or maybe he could, but it was too horrible to contemplate.

Or maybe his mind was protesting because she wasn't his daughter, yet he was fighting for her as if she were.

He snapped back to the present. "Tell me about the intimidation."

Penny and Vicki shrank a little.

"Then explain," he continued, "why you're suddenly not afraid to tell me the story."

Penny said, "Well…" She exchanged nervous glances with Vicki, then continued, "It started right after Detective Keene visited the first time. Almost as soon as she left. Somebody called my cell phone and told me never to say another word to her, or I'd get my throat cut."

"I found a note on my windshield," Vicki said. "Same thing. I got calls later, though."

"And pictures, remember?" Penny added. "Pictures of us going about our day."

"They wanted us to know they were watching," Vicki explained.

Stiletto nodded. "Sure."

"We told the cops what was going on and that was it," Penny said, her voice trailing off. She swallowed. "As for why we're here, you're not a cop, and Shelly always said—" She stopped, a little of the color draining from her skin.

"What?"

"That maybe somebody not connected with everything

could solve her problem."

The words hit hard but he kind of expected them.

She was a victim who needed a champion.

There was no longer any sense dwelling on it. Only one thing to do now—get the diary and see what Shelly had to say.

And be the champion in death she never had in life.

Stiletto sat at the counter at Chloe's, half his mind on Shelly's diary, the other half on Chloe. She'd said hello when he arrived and served his meal, but didn't say much else. Nor did she say much to her regulars.

When one of the waitresses brought Stiletto a refill of Coke, he asked, "Is Chloe okay?"

"She had a phone call earlier that upset her," the girl explained. "We're all giving her space tonight."

Stiletto said thanks and ate another piece of steak. The meat had gone cold. He'd been reading too much but had no further clues.

The bell over the diner's entrance dinged and heavy soles knocked on the floor. When Stiletto heard a throaty voice ask for black coffee, he knew Boskowictz had arrived. He didn't turn his head. He closed Shelly's diary and finished his meal.

Chloe came over and asked, "All done?" as she started to take the plate away.

"What's on your mind tonight?" he inquired.

"I should ask you." Her glance shifted to the diary and back to Stiletto.

"That belonged to Shelly," he told her. He had picked up the diary from the safe deposit box before coming to the diner.

Chloe let out a sigh. "Monica, my daughter, called a few hours ago."

"Shouldn't that be good news?"

"She was drunk or high or something. It wasn't much of a chat."

"What did she say?"

Chloe started to turn away.

"Hey."

She looked back at Stiletto.

"I'll have a big slice of apple pie for dessert," he said.

Chloe smiled and carried the plate into the kitchen. Stiletto wanted to light a cigar, but the NO SMOKING sign wasn't Chloe's idea, it was complying with city policy, so he ignored the urge.

Behind him, Boskowictz ordered meatloaf. Stiletto opened Shelly's diary again.

Presently, Chloe returned with the pie, but Stiletto didn't notice. She set the plate down. "Anybody home?"

Stiletto looked over the top of the book, his lips pressed tightly together. He set it down and cracked a smile that put a gleam in his eyes.

"Now it's my turn to ask."

"I've been talking to some people who knew Shelly,"

he said, updating her. She propped a hip on the counter and listened. When Stiletto finished, she said, "I don't believe it."

"And I've just found something that I think will put me on the killers' trail."

"What?"

Stiletto shook his head. "Too long to explain now." He pulled the pie with its whipped cream closer. "I'm going to enjoy this."

"I didn't mean to be rude earlier," she said.

"Want to talk about it?"

"Later," she replied.

Stiletto ate some pie. Chloe detached from the counter and shared a few words with Boskowictz, but Stiletto paid no attention.

The series of numbers he had found on an entire back page of Shelly's diary occupied his thoughts, and he looked at them again. She hadn't even written on half the pages in the diary, Stiletto noticed. Why fill up an entire back page? But he recognized her code for what it was. A few quiet hours in his hotel room, and he'd have the numbers deciphered.

He ate the pie slowly, his thoughts blocking out the other sounds around him until a heavy finger crashed twice into his left shoulder.

Stiletto turned his head. Boskowictz stood there, working a toothpick through his molars. His badge shined as if he polished it with the cries of beaten suspects.

Stiletto asked, "Enjoy your meatloaf?"

"Some advice, pal. Leave the police work to the police."

Stiletto stared at the other man. Boskowictz switched the toothpick from one side of his mouth to the other.

"Hear me, pal?"

Chloe took slow, deliberate breaths as her eyes bounced between the two men.

"Sure," Stiletto replied.

Boskowictz let out a short laugh, thanked Chloe for the meal, and exited the restaurant.

Chloe leaned against the counter next to Stiletto. "I want to punch him sometimes."

"Can't imagine why."

"How about some tea on the house?"

They moved to a corner booth. Chloe poured cream into her coffee while Stiletto steeped the tea bag.

"What did Monica say when she called?" he asked.

Chloe took a deep breath as she placed the empty creamer packs on the saucer. "I couldn't understand most of it. Not like this was the first time that happened. She tried telling me something, gave up, and slammed the phone down." She sipped some coffee. "I still don't know where she is."

"At least she's trying. She's still alive."

Chloe turned and stared out the window beside them. "At least there's that."

Silence lingered between them. After a while, Stiletto

asked, "What's up with Boskowictz?"

"Carl doesn't like anybody," she explained. "At least, that's what he wants people to think. He's been a friend of my family's for ages. Used to get me these huge teddy bears for Christmas. They were bigger than me; must have had a million of them. But after Shelly, he flipped. I told you my father didn't want me involved in her group. Carl didn't like it either, and told me so."

"What did he say?"

"Nothing. Stupid stuff. Just wanted to cause trouble."

Stiletto looked thoughtful and sipped his tea. He put down the mug and stirred in some sugar.

"I thought you liked it plain?" Chloe asked.

"Little sugar sounded nice."

He smiled. She smiled, too.

CHAPTER TEN

Boskowictz drove a few blocks, pulled over, and took out his cell phone. He punched in a number. Three rings. The line clicked. "Yes?" a man said.

"It's me," Boskowictz said. "I got something big."

"Chloe's friend?"

"Yes, Chloe's friend. I followed him today. Remember the Jane Doe your daughter got involved with? He's talking to the reporter and Erin and Chloe. Ben? He has her goddamn diary."

Silence on the other end.

"You hear me?"

"I heard you, Carl," Giordana said softly.

"He's going to stick his neck in our business."

"Thanks for calling, Carl."

"That's it?"

"I said—"

Boskowictz snapped a curse and ended the call.

Stiletto sat on the reclining chair. Only the nightstand lamp illuminated the otherwise dark room. He had left a pen and notepad on the table. A few scribbles on the pad represented his attempt at decoding Shelly's numbers in the back of the diary. He couldn't stay with it, though, instead flipping back through the pages, taking in the words and stories, hearing Shelly's voice as he read.

He read how excited she had been at meeting Chad through friends at work, fell in love, and felt ready to follow him wherever he wanted to go. She wrote about friends, job troubles, and her thoughts on her parents. He skipped those pages. He didn't want to know. He didn't want to discover she hated her father, and then wonder if that had been why his own daughter had broken off contact with him. He kept reading until he reached the blank pages in the back. Just like that, she was gone.

He closed the diary, stood, and paced the room, breathing deep. He found himself upset, not only over Shelly, but also the parts of his own life that he had missed, assuming they would be there when he was ready. Was he too far gone to enjoy friends? A new spouse, maybe? Finally reconcile with his daughter, Felicia?

He stopped and stared at the closed drapes. He'd had a chance at a normal life once, and it had been taken from him.

He went back to the diary and worked on the numbers some more. Numbers and letters. It made no sense on the surface, but by assuming each number and letter corresponded with a different letter of the alphabet, eventually he worked out the passage.

She had gone to a night club to interview for a job and met a man named Roger Ivey and his son, Peter. The son was quite charming, she said, and she wondered if she could get something going with him and leave Chad.

Leave Chad.

Was there a connection there? Had she tried to hide her feelings from Chad, and he'd found out anyway?

But then, how did that explain his fate? A murderer on the run always leaves traces. There was no trace of Chad Mendoza.

Stiletto put the diary down and went to the safe. He couldn't let emotion get in the way, but he was angry and looking for somebody to hit as hard as he could. The tactical side of his brain, though, nixed that idea and substituted another.

He opened the safe, took out the .45 and shoulder holster, and put the harness on. The weight of the gun on his left side felt good. His jacket covered the weapon perfectly.

Key card in his pocket, he left the room.

Stiletto told the cab driver to drop him off two blocks from his destination. He started walking. It wasn't much of a precaution. If any cameras at the club captured Stiletto's image, how he arrived wouldn't be questioned.

But his operator's mind was taking over, and you never went right to a target's front door. The camera problem was something Stiletto couldn't solve, so he didn't spend time thinking about it. If the police came after him, he knew how to hide, so he spent his time thinking about that instead.

He passed one closed establishment after another, his footsteps echoing on the sidewalk. A car went by now and then, but the street was mostly empty, the shadows crawling across the ground making his hair stand up. The jacket kept most of him warm, but his exposed neck felt the night's cold bite.

Homeless people sleeping in doorways didn't bother him. He'd seen it all before.

When he reached Roger Ivy's club, named CLUB IVY after himself, Stiletto moved across the street to a recessed doorway and melted into the shadows. The door had no label, and rust coated the lock. The hard brick building had a layer of grime, but he wasn't going to live there. The club still had some lights on inside, although the party had ended a few hours ago.

A few cars were parked along the curb in front of the club, with a space left for a fire hydrant, and Stiletto figured the night crew was still inside cleaning up. Would Ivy be there? He was taking a big chance if he wasn't.

A sign that advised of more parking in the rear of the building caught his attention, and Stiletto left the doorway to go farther down the block until he could cross the street, go up one block, and work his way to the rear of the club. The small parking area contained three cars. A light over the rear door flickered on and off at random intervals. Stiletto walked to the door, the pit of his stomach sinking a little. At the light, he reached for the bulb and gave it a twist. It went out. Stiletto once again melted into the shadows of the rear wall and waited. He took out the .45 and let the wooden grip warm in his right hand.

As Stiletto stood still, his eyes moving in a left-to-right scan, his breathing returned to normal, and the night's chill became worse. He shivered despite the jacket. When the rear door finally opened, his heart rate spiked, but he kept his body loose and ready for action.

Two women, chatting, looking behind them as they exited, saying good-night to somebody inside, and crossed the blacktop to their vehicles. The door remained open, light from the inside casting the shadow of a man on the ground. Roger Ivy watched until the women had safely departed.

The beater cars started and drove away, and the door started to swing closed. Stiletto sprang from hiding, pulling the door open, and Roger Ivy gasped as it suddenly left his grip. Stiletto stabbed the snout of the Colt into Ivy's face, the dark muzzle less than an inch from his nose.

"Back inside."

CHAPTER ELEVEN

Ivy put up his hands. "Just relax," he said.

"Back."

Ivy stepped backward, hands up, eyes on Stiletto. Scott shut the door behind him. They stood in a hallway. The warmth inside felt good, but Stiletto's right hand, the one holding the gun, still felt cold.

"Just relax," Ivy said again. "I'm not going to argue with you." The club owner spoke calmly and didn't appear nervous, although his eyes never left the dark snout of the Colt .45 auto.

"Who else is left?" Scott asked.

"The two women were the last. It's just the two of us. My office is behind me, and I have the cash there."

"I don't want cash."

Ivy blinked. "Then what are you here for?"

"Shelly Pierce."

The color drained from Ivy's face.

The coolness Ivy had demonstrated upon seeing the

gun in Stiletto's hand vanished; the man was visibly nervous.

"I-I didn't hurt her."

"We'll see about that," Stiletto told him. "Let's see your office. Walk backward."

Roger Ivy followed Stiletto's order, checking over his shoulder every few steps. He backed through a door in the hall. His office was small and cluttered, and the cash he'd referred to was stacked on the desk.

"Sit down. Hands on the desk, palms down."

Ivy obeyed. His hands shook. He watched Stiletto expectantly.

"Shelly's diary said she interviewed for a job here."

"Yes," Ivy said.

"She thought your son was cute."

"Yes."

"Talk. Fill in the gaps."

"I don't know what you want."

"Tell me what happened. Why didn't you hire her?" The Colt autoloader didn't waver.

"I was going to hire her," Ivy explained, "but she backed out."

"Why?"

"She told my son her boyfriend was getting in the way. Didn't want her working here."

"Did she say why?"

"No."

"And that was the last time you saw her?"

"Until she showed up on the news."

Stiletto's face tightened. Ivy pressed his hands harder onto the desktop, leaning forward. "I told you I didn't hurt her. Neither did my son."

"Did you go to the police?"

"My kid tried. Then he was run off the road one night. The other driver pulled my son out of his car, punched him so hard he cracked a rib, and told him to shut up about Shelly. After that, we kept quiet."

"I want to talk to your son."

"I think you should, too," Ivy said.

"Where is he?"

"Should be at home. He can be here in twenty minutes."

A telephone sat on the desk, and Stiletto gestured to it with the .45. Ivy slowly moved a shaking hand to the handset and dialed a number. He spoke to somebody, obviously his wife, telling her to wake Peter and get him on the phone because he had an urgent question. Ivy looked at Stiletto while he waited. Stiletto's arm was getting tired from holding the pistol, but he kept it pointed at Ivy's face, although the man posed no threat and was cooperating.

Stiletto decided he was sending a message that was no longer required. He put the gun back under his jacket, but he did not sit down. He left his hands on his hips. Take it easy. Don't let emotions get in the way.

I'm like this because Shelly could have been my daughter.

She isn't. Don't go crazy over "what ifs."

Scott took a deep breath and tried to steady his nerves.

Ivy swallowed and seemed to relax as he started talking again. He didn't feed "Peter" a story. He told him flat out, "Remember Shelly? There's a man here looking for some answers. I need you to come down to the club right away."

Apparently, that was all it took. Ivy told his son to come in through the back door and put the phone down.

"He's on his way."

Stiletto moved to the wall on his left and pressed his back against it.

"We aren't going to make any trouble," Ivy told him. "We've already been threatened enough."

"Did they come for you too?"

"Just my kid," Ivy said. "Erin visited me here, but I told her to go away. She knew about the hit-and-run. She told me other witnesses had been threatened, too. I told her to come back when she'd made an arrest and we'd talk. Haven't heard from her since."

Stiletto said nothing and took a deep breath. Ivy kept his hands flat on the desk. They were silent for almost a half-hour. Stiletto didn't think small talk was appropriate. What do you do on weekends? Ever hike along the Snake River? I get seasick being on water, but I don't mind looking at it.

When the rear door squeaked open, Ivy called, "In the office, Peter."

Stiletto snatched out his pistol and held it ready.

"You don't need that."

Stiletto ignored him. The young man who came through the doorway stopped short, eyes widening. "Whoa," he said, putting up his hands.

"Sit down. Turn the chair so it faces me."

Peter Ivy wore wrinkled clothes and his hair was uncombed, face and eyes still clouded with sleep. He did as he was told; he moved the chair in front of his father's desk to the wall opposite Stiletto and sat down.

"Keep your hands on your knees," Stiletto told him.

Peter Ivy nodded and complied.

Stiletto put away the pistol.

"Shelly Pierce," he said. "I want to know who killed her."

"Okay."

"Tell me what you know."

"Why?"

"Peter," Roger Ivy cautioned.

"I just told you," Stiletto said.

"But who are you? You aren't a cop."

"Nope."

"You a Fed?"

"Peter!"

"I just want to know, Dad. What's the big deal?"

"He's not from around here. That makes him different from Erin and everybody else."

Stiletto said to the young man, "You want to get even

with the guy who punched you, right?"

Peter Ivy felt along the left side of his ribcage. "Sure."

"Tell me about Shelly."

Peter dropped his eyes for a moment. "Well, I really liked her. She wasn't happy with the guy she was with."

"Chad?"

"Yeah. I thought I could steal her away."

"Did she say anything about some friends Chad had?"

Peter looked up. "Oh, yeah. She hated them. She called them the 'frat boys.'"

"Why didn't she like them?"

"She called them a bunch of crooks."

"Why?"

"Because she said they stole stuff. They were their own little Wild Bunch, you know? Like in the movies."

"Was that what Chad told her?" Stiletto said.

"I don't know what he told her. He was trying to get out."

"Why?"

"The boss of the gang was pushing them too hard. He wanted bigger scores, bigger money, all that. He was saying that if they had to hurt somebody along the way, they should do that."

"Who was this boss?"

"She said his name was Damien."

"They stole stuff, and what else?"

"You mean, like drugs?"

"I mean, like drugs, yeah."

"I don't know, man. Shelly never said anything about that." He paused for a moment, but his eyes communicated there was more he wanted to say.

"What are you not telling me, Peter?"

"Well, when Shelly and I got to hang out, it was because Chad was gone."

"Gone where?"

"Something to do with the gang. Shelly didn't know what, but she said they had something on the north side of town near the Snake River."

"A hideout?"

"I don't know, man. Maybe if they were into drugs and that's where they kept them."

Stiletto nodded. It was similar to what Shelly's friends had said at the café, but the mention of Chad wanting out was new. The "hideout" was new too, whatever that meant. Was Chad killed, and Shelly killed, because he wanted to leave the gang?

"Any idea where I can find this gang? This so-called 'Wild Bunch?'"

Peter glanced at his father.

Roger Ivy said, "If you know, you should tell him."

Peter raised his eyes to Stiletto.

"Shipwreck Bar. At least that's where they used to go. I don't know if they still do."

"What's special about that place?"

"It's out of the main area of town. They use the loft above the bar as a hangout. Or used to. Like I said, I don't know if they still do. Maybe they changed to the other place."

Stiletto let the silence linger in the office for a moment, then turned to the father.

"I apologize for barging in here and waving a gun around."

"If you can find who killed Shelly," Roger Ivy said, "all's forgiven."

"I'll find the killer," Stiletto said. He started for the door. "No doubt."

The son asked, "What was she to you?"

Stiletto paused in the doorway and looked at the young man. He figured Peter Ivy deserved an answer, and Scott honestly wanted to give one.

But now wasn't the time.

"It would take too long to explain," Scott said.

"Hey!" Peter Ivy said, "I told you everything. Now you owe us."

Stiletto said, "I'm doing a favor for a friend who doesn't know Shelly's dead."

"Why isn't your friend here?"

"Because he died a few days ago."

"What—"

Roger Ivy said, "Peter, that's enough."

The younger man fell silent.

Stiletto said good-bye, left father and son in the office, and returned to the street.

He had a lot to talk to Detective Erin Keene about the next time he crossed her path.

But that wasn't the only thing on his mind.

Scott walked in the chill of the night for a long time.

CHAPTER TWELVE

Breakfast the next morning was scrambled eggs, a thick slice of ham, and a pot of tea with a glass of orange juice on the side delivered by room service. Stiletto ate by the window, but the drapes remained closed. He wasn't ready to open them, and the deeper he delved into the Shelly situation, the more he wanted to keep them closed forever.

He left the TV off. He wanted to find out if the news was reporting anything of the goings-on in Venezuela after the overthrow of the old government. He wanted to know if his friends there were okay, but he knew the American media would be focused on problems in the US and the usual political machinations in Washington, DC that seemed to mean so much in the moment but amounted to very little in the grand scheme. Politicians came and went. Policies hit or missed. One guy started a program, and the next guy changed it or ended it. Stiletto was more interested in the aspects of US politics that never changed, and should never change—life, liberty, the pursuit of happiness, and the opposition, violent or otherwise, of those who stood in the way.

He opened a sketchbook. As an Army brat who had trouble making friends when he was young, Scott had taught himself how to draw in response to always moving with his father's various postings around the world. He still drew, and the Zen-like practice meant more to him now than it ever had.

He sat at the table with the dirty dishes pushed aside and scratched a dark pencil across the page. Within an hour, he had a picture. The face of a young girl.

He gave her big oval eyes and colored in the pupils so they were dark like the eyes on many Italian women he had known. He added long, flowing hair and curled the ends. Finally, he added a half-open mouth, as if the girl was getting ready to say something.

When he finished, he stared at the drawing.

He wondered what the girl was going to say.

He wondered what he was going to say back.

But they only stared at each other. Neither could communicate.

Stiletto pulled the page from the sketchbook and tore it apart in disgust. Then he sat and stared at the floor for a long time.

The Shipwreck Bar lived up to its name.

The neon sign flickered, and the neon ship adjacent to the sign wasn't lit at all. A food truck was parked out front, next to a cluster of smokers on the sidewalk.

Having engaged a rental car now that the search was heating up, Stiletto shook his head as he drove by. The darkened second level on top of the building might still be occupied. There was no way to tell, but the rest of the bar wasn't overly exciting. He'd seen plenty of dive bars over the years, and while the Shipwreck might not resemble the worst of them, it wasn't the best of a bad lot, either.

Maybe the inside would be better.

He continued along Kimberly Road past a variety of businesses, including restaurants, auto shops, and storage places. He turned right onto Locust, passing the side of the bar, where cars were parked. More smokers clustered by the side door, on which hung a sign that said EXIT in bright neon letters. At least that sign was working. Stiletto slowed the Ford, parked off the road near the corner of 2nd Avenue, and went back on foot.

He wasn't used to small towns. A lot of open space existed between the various establishments, and the openness made the hair on the back of Stiletto's neck tingle. There were plenty of open lots between structures, and that meant plenty of areas where an ambush might await. He had a plan in mind for his visit to the Shipwreck, but the plan called for kicking a hornet's nest. If what Peter Ivy had said was true, the hornets were inside the Shipwreck Bar and deserved a good kicking. His conversation with

Peter Ivy replayed in a constant loop. A team of crooks. A wild bunch, yeah. A bunch of punks who weren't above murdering two people to keep their crimes a secret.

And then there was the syndicate question. Was the gang part of a bigger operation or protected by the bigger operation? Why? Who covered up their crimes?

What crime had they killed Shelly and Chad to protect? Was it an on-going venture or a one-time deal, long finished?

Stiletto's shoes crunched on the loose gravel. There was no sidewalk here, only blacktop, divided from the road by a small dip for runoff. Sewer grates were spaced out along the dip. Headlamps from passing cars flashed in Stiletto's eyes, but he ignored them despite his inclination to run for a dark corner and seek cover. There was nobody hunting him in Twin Falls, Idaho.

At least, not yet.

After tonight, that might change.

Unless Peter Ivy had been lying.

Then he'd go back to the young man and have an entirely different conversation with him.

He passed the side parking area. The smokers took no notice of him, but he heard their chatter as he walked by. He didn't want to go in through the side.

There was a dirt plot instead of pavement at the entrance to the Shipwreck, and Scott kicked up a little dust as he reached the front steps and pushed inside.

Loud music, louder conversation, and a darkened

interior greeted him like a slap in the face, along with a blast of pent-up body heat from the crush of individuals inside. Wood floor and wood-paneled walls. Long bar, well-stocked. Jukebox in one corner, and booths in the very back. No tables. Most of the patrons were at the bar, while others encircled the trio of pool tables. The juke wasn't blasting country music as Scott might have predicted, but heavy metal riffs instead, the kind of hard-rocking, hard-pumping music that made you want to punch somebody—preferably whoever put on the record. Stiletto actually enjoyed heavy metal, but the amount the juke was pumping out, along with the high volume, was close to overdose levels.

If there was a way to access the upper loft from the bar, Stiletto couldn't see it from the doorway.

He took a spot at the bar that was vacated by a couple who took their beer mugs to an empty pool table. The two bartenders, a short man and a tall woman, hustled along the bar, filling orders. It took a few minutes, but Stiletto finally caught the male bartender's attention.

"Makers and Coke," Stiletto told him.

The bartender nodded, filled a glass, and set it on a napkin in front of Scott. He moved to the next customer, an already inebriated female who tried coming onto him along with asking for a reload on her Cosmo. Her slurred flirting made the female bartender, close enough to over-hear, laugh, and she filled a beer mug from a tap.

Stiletto might as well have been invisible for all the attention he received as he sipped his drink, the ice clinking against the glass. The mix was stronger than Stiletto normally poured on his own, but it tasted good.

Now what? He wanted to show Shelly's picture around and ask who had seen her in an attempt to draw out the "wild bunch," but with the crowd and the loud music, he wasn't sure that was the best course of action. When a corner table behind him opened, Stiletto moved to that spot to watch the action. He finished his drink and flagged down a waitress for a refill.

Maybe waiting until the crowd thinned was a better approach.

Maybe waiting for whoever lived upstairs to return was even better.

Stiletto realized there was no rush.

He had plenty of time.

CHAPTER THIRTEEN

"Have you seen this girl?"

Stiletto presented the waitress with Shelly Pierce's picture on the third refill of Makers & Coke.

"Never seen her," the waitress said, quickly starting to turn away.

"Look again."

The waitress said, "I'm busy," and hustled away.

Stiletto wasn't surprised. He put the picture away. She was the only person on the floor chasing orders. She hadn't dropped her eyes to the picture at all. No sense chalking her reaction up to conspiracy yet.

Stiletto remained seated, nursing his third drink, eventually switching to ice water. He was feeling the effects of the bourbon a little. It had been a while since his last drink, and since he didn't partake of alcoholic beverages as much as he used to, the alcohol hit him harder than he'd counted on. Not hard enough to keep him from accomplishing his task, though.

More eyes snapped his way as time went on, everybody probably wondering who the dude in the corner was, and why was he watching everybody. None of the looks were obvious, simply concealed curiosity. When several patrons wandered out after midnight, thinning the herd a little, Stiletto left the table. He leaned against the bar and put Shelly's picture on the polished top.

"Refill?" the man asked. His female counterpart had gone home an hour before.

"Seen this girl?"

The bartender said, "You a cop?"

"No. Seen her?"

The bartender at least looked, glancing at the photo long enough to shake his head, lift his eyes to Stiletto, and say, "No, man." With that, he moved on to the next customer.

Stiletto went down the bar a little, asking the same question, and then the bartender told him to quit bothering customers and get out if he wasn't going to order anything. Perhaps Peter Ivy had not told the whole truth. Perhaps Stiletto had expected too much. Maybe this wasn't the lead he had thought it would be.

The bartender's hostile eyes remained on Stiletto while he stood making up his mind. He wanted to resist enough to spark the bartender into further action, should he be working for the wild bunch in keeping trouble away from the bar. Eventually, Stiletto turned for the door and stepped outside, but not before he stole one more look back to see the bartender lifting a telephone from under the bar.

The food truck had departed, but the air was still full of cigarette smoke from the cluster of men and women taking a smoke break outside. Stiletto stepped away from the group and took out the Davidoff Escurio Corona Gorda he'd purchased with his Upmanns. Clipping the end, he took his time lighting up, casting a sideways glance at the loft above the bar. Lights were on behind the windows now. How had the occupants returned to the loft? There wasn't a side entrance on the lower level.

The cigarette gang looked at him as his thick cigar smoke drifted their way, but nobody said anything. The chatter continued, most of the words silly young people's talk. The concerns of the young were amusing. They were out of college or trade school or none of the above, trying to make their way in the world, and talking about the struggles and discoveries that were unique to no one but seemed so to them. Minor problems—annoyances, really—seemed like major obstacles. After listening for about ten minutes, Stiletto wanted to go over and tell them not to worry, everything will work out by the time you're forty.

But they wouldn't want to hear that. And he'd ruin their self-discovery. He remained quiet and enjoyed the hearty flavor of the Davidoff.

The bartender quickly dialed a number. He knew the stranger had seen him pick up the phone and had an idea the stranger knew what he was doing, but he didn't care. He had an establishment to take care of and didn't need the trouble the stranger was bringing.

The line connected to the loft upstairs.

The bartender spoke quickly to the person who answered, explaining that somebody was here asking about "that girl" and maybe somebody might want to do something about him. The person on the other end hung up.

The bartender set the phone down and put the call out of his mind as another customer ordered a drink. With a smile, he started filling a glass.

The cigar had barely burned the first inch when a car pulled off the road and stopped in the dirt in front of the bar. The dust cloud didn't scatter the smokers, but they did shift a little closer to the building. The car, Stiletto noted, was a new Dodge Challenger. Gray in color, and judging from its deep grumble, equipped with a powerful motor. The car shut off. The driver did not exit. Tinted windows prevented Scott from seeing inside.

Stiletto puffed on his cigar. The Davidoff was an expensive cigar that he didn't usually smoke, and he saw no reason to spend a ton of money on a single cigar when it really wasn't any better than an H. Upmann or one of his other preferred brands. The smoke flavor was smooth, but not forty-dollar-a-stick smooth.

Three men stepped out of the bar.

The driver of the Challenger swung open the door and stepped out, then gently pushed it shut. He was tall and bulky, a man who spent a lot of time at the gym. He matched the description of "Damien" provided by Shelly's friends.

The smokers glanced at the men on the front steps and maintained their composure, but they also hurriedly stomped out their cigarettes and headed back inside. The three men at the front door parted to let them pass.

The bar's door swung shut.

Stiletto let out a stream of smoke.

The Challenger's driver, dark-haired, broad-shouldered, wearing a t-shirt and jeans, kicked at a rock and started toward Scott.

"Somebody's sticking his nose where it doesn't belong."

Stiletto laughed.

"Did I say something funny?"

Scott looked at the man. Twenty-something. Bony jaw, hot eyes. He stopped with only a few feet between him and Stiletto. Scott quickly judged the distance.

"Are you Damien?"

"What's it to you?"

Stiletto lifted his right leg and kicked Damien in the stomach. The young man let out a hoarse yell, doubling over. Stiletto stepped forward to grab a handful of his thick dark hair and wrenched his head up. He jammed the lit end of the Davidoff into Damien's exposed neck, the skin searing for a split second. Damien's eyes rolled into the back of his head as he tried to scream and breathe at the same time.

Stiletto swept Damien's legs out from under him and let the man fall to the dirt. Stepping over the moaning body, Scott braced to fight the remaining three.

Two hesitated but stood their ground. The third ran to the wall behind him, where empty beer bottles had been placed on a brick ledge. He grabbed one, smashed it against the wall, and gripped the jagged remains by the neck.

Stiletto balled a fist and met the first thug with a right cross, spinning him like a top. He fell against one of his buddies, who stumbled into Stiletto's raised right knee. His head snapped back, and Scott followed through with a kick to his chest. Another one down. Then Bottle Man lunged.

CHAPTER FOURTEEN

Bottle Man swung the jagged edge at Scott's chest, the glass barely touching the fabric of Stiletto's shirt.

Stiletto stepped back, dodging the inert bodies on the ground while yelling, "Come on! Try harder!"

A dust cloud kicked up by the furious movements surrounded Stiletto and his young opponent, who coughed as he sucked a mouthful of it into his mouth. Stiletto knocked the bottle out of the man's hand and it shattered on the ground, then he threw a right. The man blocked it. His forearm was solid muscle, and Stiletto felt a jolt of pain through his fist. The man countered with a right of his own, socking Scott in the jaw. Stiletto ignored the hit and stepped into the man's next swing, hammering a hard double-blow into his solar plexus. The man fell back gasping, coughing, and retching.

Two police cars, minus lights and sirens, screeched to a stop in front of the bar. Spotlights hit Stiletto directly. He lifted an arm to block the glare as officers sprang from the patrol cars with drawn guns.

"Get on the ground! Get on the ground now!"

Stiletto dropped to his knees with his hands behind his head.

"I said on the ground!"

Stiletto spat blood. His lower lip was bleeding. He stretched down in the dust.

Two officers ran to him, slapping cuffs on his wrists and binding his arms behind his back. He grunted at the strain on his back and arms but kept his mouth shut. The two officers grabbed him by the elbows and half-carried, half-dragged him toward their patrol car, where they let him drop in front of the bumper.

Scott managed a look back. The other two officers were helping the wild bunch to their feet and using the radio to call for an ambulance.

One of the cops near Stiletto kicked dust into Scott's face.

"The hell you lookin' at?"

Stiletto coughed, spat, and turned his face away.

There was a commotion of voices from the wild bunch, the cop in charge sorting the story into a coherent narrative. One of the thugs said, "Call my old man and he'll fix this."

"Who's your old man?" the lead cop said.

"Doug Armstrong."

"Sure."

The cops brought out the bartender, who identified

Scott as "the dude causing trouble" and the cops said okay. When the ambulance arrived, the four goons were treated for their injuries, and the lead cop said they should go to the hospital for a full check-up. They didn't argue. The ambulance carried them away.

Then it was only Scott and the cops.

The lead officer came over to the two cops guarding Stiletto and said, "Stuff him in back. Let's get him booked."

They lifted Stiletto again and forcefully jammed him into the back of their patrol car. Stiletto kept his mouth shut. His jaw hurt, and his lip leaked blood that trickled down his chin.

The best-laid plans of mice and men, et cetera. Stiletto wondered exactly what kind of mess he'd fallen into as the police car took off down the road.

Stiletto was booked at the city jail and placed in a holding cell. A bench wound around the square room. The walls were bare white, the lights fluorescent and bright. The room was filled with other individuals lucky enough to score a night at the gray-bar hotel with all expenses paid. Most were drunk. Others sat quietly with defeated expressions. Nobody looked at him. Stiletto found a spot on a bench placed against a bare wall and sat quietly too.

His plan had been to get the wild bunch in the open. Success. Peter Ivy had told the truth. Next, he wanted them disabled and ready for interrogation. Fail. He wondered why the one thug had mentioned his father. Was he counting on special treatment because of a family member connected to the city government? Or connected to something more nefarious?

The cops had fingerprinted him and taken his belongings, including Shelly's picture. It wouldn't take long to find out who he was, but his former status as a soldier and government employee wouldn't mean anything to the officers. Could Chloe post bail? Would he even be granted bail? Were those thugs connected enough, and shielded enough, that the judge would keep Stiletto locked up?

He had no idea what he was going to do next. His only option was to make it up as he went along.

One of the drunks threw up in the corner. Stiletto covered his mouth and nose as the stench hit him.

Two officers opened the door of the holding cell and one called Stiletto's name.

Scott wanted to show some restraint upon his exit, but the vomit in the corner was overpowering, and he left the bench as if somebody had put a match under his backside.

One of the cops cuffed him, and together they marched Stiletto down a bland hallway to an interview room. The number 2 was stenciled on the heavy steel door. They left him in a steel chair, wrists still cuffed. He sat uncomfortably but continued to keep his mouth closed. The cops left.

The room was cold, with more bare walls and glaring fluorescent light. The table in front of Scott had gouge marks and scratches on the surface. The empty chair opposite was also made of steel. Scott sat with his head lowered, his eyes darting around.

He was in big trouble and knew it. There was nothing to do except wait for a bail hearing and get back on the street that way, but the last thing he needed was cops dogging his trail when he skipped. He didn't have the CIA to help him make such problems go away any longer.

The steel door behind him swung open and crashed against the wall. Stiletto jumped in surprise.

The door shut with finality.

"You're lucky I got here first."

Stiletto jerked his head around.

CHAPTER FIFTEEN

Detective Erin Keene walked to the other side of the table, pulled the opposite chair out, and dropped into it. She still wore her jean jacket. No make-up. She looked more tired than the last time he'd seen her, but her eyes focused sharply on Stiletto's face.

"I happened to be working the late shift tonight," she said. "When I saw your name on the booking sheet, I ran down from upstairs."

"Uh-huh."

"Otherwise you're on the way to the meat grinder. Somebody called Boskowictz to come and talk to you, and I think you know what that means."

"Uh-huh."

"What happened?"

"Are you speaking for the cops or yourself?"

"I'm asking for us."

Stiletto frowned. He wasn't expecting a line like that. He said, "I went to the Shipwreck Bar looking for a lead on who killed Shelly Pierce."

"Did you find one?"

"I got some names, yeah."

"The men you tangled with?"

"My source told me those four men are involved in some sort of criminal activity. Shelly's boyfriend, Chad, was part of the group. I think Chad or Shelly or both either saw or heard something they shouldn't have, and the crew killed them."

"What names do you have?"

"Damien is the leader. No last name."

"And?"

"One of them tonight said his father was Doug Armstrong. Does that mean anything to you?"

"Not off the top of my head. Were they brought in, too?"

"Cops loaded them into an ambulance and they went away. You'll have to check the hospitals."

"You beat them so bad they had to go to the hospital?"

"Damien will be easy to find," Stiletto said. "I jammed a lit cigar into his neck."

Erin's eyes didn't leave Stiletto's face. She sat, stunned, blinking several times.

"I'll call around," she said. "You don't believe in subtle, do you?"

"No."

"All right, listen," she said, "we can't talk here. The good news is nobody has filed charges, so I can get you out of here. When Boskowictz finally leaves whatever poker game or strip club he's hanging out at, he's going to want to know where you are. I'll fake him out. Been doing it for years. You need to get back to your hotel and maybe find another place to hang out in the meantime."

Stiletto nodded.

"Can you memorize?"

"Sure."

She gave him her address. "Swing by later, and we'll talk some more. Who's your source?"

"Nope."

"Had to ask. Let's get you out of those cuffs and out the door before the sharks arrive."

The legs of her chair scraped on the floor as she stood up. Stiletto straightened in his seat while she unlocked his handcuffs. He massaged his wrists while she put the cuffs in the pocket of her jean jacket.

"You always wear that?" Stiletto said, standing up.

"What's it to you?"

"Just curious."

She grabbed his left elbow. "Come on."

Stiletto let her lead him out.

Carl Boskowictz placed his revolver in one of the lockers in the front section of the jail and used a keycard to enter the reception area, where two officers sat behind a desk. The holding area was a few feet away. A janitor was inside cleaning the floor, the guests having been shoved to the opposite side of the room while he worked, two guards watching from the doorway.

Boskowicz stopped at the desk. "You're holding somebody for me."

"Name?" One of the officers produced a clipboard.

"Stiletto is his name."

"He's gone, Sergeant."

"What do you mean, 'gone?'"

"Released. No charges, no witnesses."

"Who checked him out?"

The officer consulted the sheet. "Detective Keene, Sergeant."

Boskowicz cursed and shook his head. "Figures." He didn't say good-bye. He returned to the front, retrieved his revolver, and went back out to his patrol car.

With the driver's door open, his left foot out of the car on the ground, he used his cell phone to call Ben Giordana.

"It's late, Carl."

"Sorry to wake you."

"Who's sleeping?"

"No kidding. We have a problem."

"Another one?"

"Your daughter's new boyfriend got arrested tonight."

"For what?"

"For a fight at the Shipwreck Bar."

"Oh, no."

"Oh, yes," the sergeant said. "Story is he was showing Shelly Pierce's picture around and asking if anybody had seen her. The bartender called the boys, they called Damien, and they decided to take care of the issue themselves."

"What happened?"

"Stiletto turned them inside out. They're at the hospital getting patched up."

"Wow," Giordana said. "Who sprung Stiletto from jail?"

"Take a guess."

"Keene?"

"Yes, sir," Boskowictz said. "On the grounds that there are no witnesses and no charges."

"We have a big problem," Giordana said.

"We need to do something before they get too close. It would be a shame if they put Chloe in danger."

"Watch your mouth, Carl."

"I'm just telling you."

"And I'm telling you that I still call the shots around here, despite the turkey south of town. Do you understand, Carl?"

"I understand."

Ben Giordana said nothing for a moment. Boskowictz heard him breathing hard, though. The sergeant looked absently around the parking lot, then glanced at his boots. They needed a shine. He checked his watch. Another two hours on watch, then he could go home and crash.

"You still there, Ben?" the sergeant said.

"Let's take care of the issue," Giordana said. "Get it done right, though."

Boskowictz hesitated a little. The Twin Falls syndicate had lasted so long because everything was done quietly, but now he was being ordered to arrange the murders of two people, one of whom was a cop. The status quo was being upset. The big man didn't like that, but he had his orders. "I'll handle it."

Carl Boskowictz ended the call without a good-bye and stowed the cell. He chuckled as he started the car. Giordana thought he still called the shots?

Yeah, right. And the real puppet master was the reason Boskowictz had to take charge of a very unpleasant job.

CHAPTER SIXTEEN

Who could sleep?

He couldn't, that was for sure.

Ben Giordana, in his red silk bathrobe and blue pajamas, stood on the balcony of his penthouse, which overlooked the city. The nighttime chill didn't bother him.

He'd quit smoking years ago. Otherwise, he'd be smoking a Lucky Strike and letting his mind wander. Back then, solutions had been easy. Now, his mind raced with questions. He felt like a rat trapped in a maze with no way out.

He brushed his right ear. He needed a haircut, but there were more important matters on his mind.

He looked at the smartphone in his right hand and punched in a number. Two rings and the other end picked up.

"Yeah, boss?"

"Any sign of my granddaughter?"

"Got a lead in Toledo."

"Okay."

"Why you up so late, chief?"

"Problems, Vince."

"Try me."

Ben Giordana and Vince Six had known each other for decades. Six had never climbed out of the "enforcer" position, but he was Giordana's right hand. Except lately, he'd been on the road looking for Chloe's kid. Giordana didn't want to admit that he needed Six back in Twin Falls and fast.

He updated Six on the Stiletto situation and his frustration with Boskowictz.

"Carl plays both sides now, Ben."

"I know."

"What's going to happen?"

"We're going to have a dead cop and a dead snooper in the next few days. We can't have the turkey south of town getting upset."

"Aren't you tired of doing that punk's bidding?"

"We don't have much choice, Vince."

"You got lots of choices, Ben."

"I need you back here as soon as possible."

"But—"

"We'll find her later. I need you here."

"I'll get on a plane in the morning."

Giordana said okay and ended the call. He went back inside, pulled the balcony doors closed, and returned to his bedroom to try and get some rest.

"You always wear that?"

The question bounced around Detective Erin Keene's mind as she drove home.

The old jean jacket with the fraying cuffs was part of her everyday wardrobe, yeah. She was never without it for very long. It stayed home when she was out on a date or at a fancy-dress event, but otherwise, it was never far from her.

Just like the memory of the person who used to wear it, too.

She pulled into the driveway of her modest one-story home and shut off the car. She'd like to have the use of her garage, but she had accumulated a lot of crap, and the garage was where that waited until she had the time to sort everything and either toss items or sell the more valuable stuff on eBay. She had a very large collection of expensive dolls that were gaining in value every year.

Leaving the car with her purse in hand, she locked the doors and proceeded up the walk to the porch. There was a small step with her worn-out welcome mat and a set of metal animals on either side. Two Dachshunds, a cat, and a chicken. She'd grown up on a farm, and the metal caricatures reminded her of her youth. The chicken especially made her smile more often than not, since, as an energetic eight-year-old, it had been her job to gather the eggs from the hens. The Dachshunds were stand-ins for the pets she'd had during that time, Iggy and Squiggy.

She'd gone so far as to put collars on the models with the letters I and S dangling from small chains.

Key in the lock. The door opened, and she stopped short of entering to grab the mail. Locking the door behind her, she placed her keys, purse, and the mail on the entry table, then hung her jean jacket on the coat hook mounted on the wall.

She started for the kitchen with her gun still on her hip. She needed a beer. It was too early to drink, but when one worked night watch, the usual rules went straight to the trash can. A cold beer and some morning television before she went to bed sounded like a great idea.

She stopped with a gasp as she entered the kitchen.

The two men seated at the table weren't surprised at all. They were both bulky, filling out their street clothes with muscle instead of fat. One of the thugs jumped up. He had a fully-extended metal baton in his hand and a sneer on his face.

She grabbed for the Glock-19 on her hip, and the 9mm pistol filled her hand as she took the proper two-hand isosceles stance and put pressure on the trigger.

The second seated goon, who wore glasses, dived for cover under the table. Erin Keene paid him no mind as she lined up the first man in his sights, but he moved quickly, and the blunt end of the baton struck her in the belly sooner than she'd expected. Her breath rushed out as pain filled her midsection, the Glock firing as the trigger locked back but the bullet striking the top of the stove instead of its intended target.

Erin dropped to her knees. Sucking air in short gasps, she tried to rise. Rolling to the side was out of the question. The kitchen was too narrow for that kind of maneuver. She brought up her gun halfway, but the baton swung again, crashing against her wrist. Fire spread along the length of her arm. She cried out again and fell back against the lower cabinet.

The second goon emerged from cover. He didn't have a gun. Instead, he flexed very large hands.

"Pick her up," said the first man.

The big man with the wire-framed spectacles reached for her. She had no power to resist.

Stiletto caught a cab from the jail, and the driver brought him back to where he'd left the rental. They passed the now-closed Shipwreck Bar along the way, and if you hadn't known there had been a fight out front, nothing left behind would indicate that there had been violence.

Scott paid the driver and slid behind the wheel of the rental. The car was unmolested and the engine fired at the twist of the key.

The sun was almost up, the sky a clear blue, birds chirping. It was almost peaceful, except for the undercurrent of corruption obviously running through the veins of the town.

He turned onto the street with a momentary thought of falling into bed at his hotel.

Then a vision of Erin Keene flashed in his mind. Stiletto didn't believe in luck, but their meeting had been a stroke of fortune, for sure. A sudden sixth sense told him to haul ass to her house.

He punched her address into the in-dash GPS and followed the voice commands carefully.

Halfway there, he wished he had the Colt .45, which was locked safely in his hotel room.

Where it did him no good at all.

Traffic wasn't bad. It was still too early for the morning rush. He reached Erin's house and parked at the curb in front. Her car sat in the driveway. Nothing seemed out of the ordinary. Maybe he was overreacting.

A gun cracked inside the house.

CHAPTER SEVENTEEN

Stiletto bolted through the yard to the door and turned the knob. Locked, of course. He stepped back and looked for something to smash the front window with, and was rewarded with a variety of metal animals. He grabbed one of the Dachshunds—it was solid—and tossed it through the window.

The metal dog punched a hole in the glass and left long spider cracks branching out from the perimeter, but it wasn't enough. Scott grabbed the chicken next. It was made of sheets of metal riveted together, but was plenty stout. The metal was cold, the layer of dust on the surface spreading to his hands as he grasped it and shoved the chicken away with both hands like a medicine ball. The chicken widened the hole, more pieces of glass falling inside and out. Stiletto grabbed the other dog and held it in one hand as he knocked more of the glass away, finally creating enough space to jump through. He hunched his back to keep from bashing into the window frame above and cutting skin or clothes on the remaining shards of glass. He landed on a couch, almost losing his balance, and leaped over the coffee table to land on the wood floor.

Entryway to his right, heavy footsteps coming his way. A man with glasses and a baton entered the room. His clothes were wet. He yelled as he lurched at Scott, raising the baton. Stiletto dodged the swing and let a right cross go, his fist flying through the air as the goon sidestepped.

The baton crashed into Stiletto's stomach. As the air rushed out of him, he doubled over. The goon kicked his right leg and Stiletto hit the floor. The goon lifted the baton again. Stiletto grabbed for the goon's right ankle and pulled hard. Off-balance, the goon fell back and struck his head solidly on the coffee table. Stiletto wasn't sure what cracked louder, the wood table or the goon's skull.

He grabbed the baton and ran down the hall, stopping in the kitchen. On the floor lay a Glock 9mm pistol, the gun that had gone off. The stove had taken the slug. There was a nice round hole in between the front burners.

A woman screamed from down the hall.

Pistol beats baton. Stiletto dropped the baton, picked up the Glock, and ran in the direction of the scream. He came to a well-decorated family room with couches, television, family pictures, and a hallway to his left. Water splashed wildly. Bathroom.

Three long steps to the first door on the right and Stiletto extended the Glock in a two-hand hold.

Another goon kneeled on the side of a full bathtub, the water splashing over as he struggled to keep a body under the water. The goon had one hand on Erin Keene's head and the other on her neck but was having a hard time with her flailing arms. The detective was not going to die without a fight.

Stiletto took the fight out of the goon with a 9mm slug to the back of his head.

The goon fell forward into the tub, Erin raising her head enough to gasp and then scream as the clear water turned red. Scott grabbed the thug by the shirt collar and hauled him out, water splashing on the tiled floor. Scott dropped the thug flat on his back, where the overhead light highlighted the gaping exit wound in the front of his head.

Erin coughed, struggling to rise. She was naked. Her clothes were on the floor, under the thug now. Black welts were already dotting her face and neck. Her eyes were glassy, and her hands kept slipping on either edge of the tub as she tried to push out of the water, splashing more out each time she tried. The thugs had hit her several times to partially knock her out, get her clothes off, and push her into the tub.

Stiletto set the Glock on the toilet lid and grabbed for her, but she scratched him as he lifted her from the water.

"It's me!" he shouted. "It's Stiletto! You're okay!"

Her wide eyes zeroed in on his face, and she stopped fighting and clung to him tightly. He carried her, dripping wet, out of the bathroom. She pointed to where her bedroom was and he went there, placing her on the bed. He ran back for two big towels. She didn't need help drying off and did so vigorously while he grabbed a bathrobe from the back of a nearby chair.

She tied the robe tightly around her waist. Her shoulders sank, and she put her hands to her face.

"Oh, my God," she said.

Stiletto tried to pull her hands away. "Let me see."

She slapped at him. "I'm fine."

"Are you?"

A pause. She dropped her hands into her lap. "No. But don't touch me. Please."

Stiletto stepped back. "Take it easy a minute. I'll get some coffee going."

She told him where to find it, and he went back to the kitchen.

Once the coffee was brewing, he checked on the goon who had landed on the coffee table. Goner. Red fluid leaked out of the crack in his head to stain the floor. He stood over the body a moment. There would be a lot of explaining to do, as in why Erin Keene had two dead goons in her home, both of whom had been killed by a man she'd released from custody?

He hoped she had allies in the department. If the cops were as dirty as he'd seen so far, he wasn't sure how far they'd get before more killers made a second attempt.

Because the enemy knew their time was up. Had Scott returned to his hotel, he might have met the same reception committee.

He poured a mug of coffee for Erin. When he brought it to her, he had to set it on the nightstand because her hands were shaking too much to hold the mug.

CHAPTER EIGHTEEN

"I take it nobody's ever tried to kill you before?"

They were on the edge of Erin Keene's bed. She hadn't moved from where she'd sat down after putting on her robe. The welts on her right cheek and neck were turning black.

"What kind of question is that?"

"Well—"

"Does it happen to you often?"

"Yes. The Russians have a contract out on me right now. I can't remember how much I'm worth."

She leaned away from him. "Who are you?"

"A good friend to have in a fight."

She relaxed again. "What made you come here?"

"A hunch."

"That's it?"

"A vision."

"Okay."

"I had a feeling I needed to be here, and I arrived in time to save your life."

She paused for a moment and let out a breath. "Thank you."

"Thank you for getting me out of jail, if I haven't said so already."

"You forgot."

Stiletto forced a laugh.

"Sorry about your window," he said.

"What did you use to break in?"

"Two dogs and a chicken."

The chuckle began in her stomach, but it didn't stay there. She let out a laugh.

At that moment, Stiletto knew she'd be okay.

She said, "Since you asked, no, nobody's ever tried to purposefully murder me before."

"We need to have a much longer conversation than our first," he said.

"Apparently, you know more than me at this point."

Stiletto rose from the bed. "Get dressed. I'll call the police. I'm surprised the commotion didn't stir the neighbors."

"In this town? Scott, everybody here keeps their head down and their mouth shut."

"I'm sorry to hear that."

He left the room and pulled the bedroom door closed behind him.

Maybe by the time he was finished in Twin Falls, the population would do more than hide when trouble happened.

Presently the cops showed up, two squad cars first, then an unmarked car with two detectives who knew Erin well. Stiletto stayed back while she answered questions. When they finally had to ask who he was and what was he doing at the house, she explained that he was her cousin, in town visiting, and arrived just as the goons dragged her into the bathroom, which forced him to break the window to get inside.

The lie wouldn't last once the detectives checked him out. They would do so as a matter of routine and would learn of his earlier arrest. He'd let Erin explain why she'd told the whopper. Maybe they would understand. She wasn't the only decent cop on the force, after all. At least, he hoped not.

The crime scene crew needed a few hours to gather their information and clear out the bodies. Erin would need to hire a specific cleaning crew for her bathroom and she decided now was the perfect time for a remodel, so she'd close it off for the time being.

Once they were done with questions and the medics had treated Erin's wounds and applied bandages, Stiletto and the detective drove to Scott's hotel. She'd made a point of grabbing her jean jacket before they departed, and Stiletto bit off asking her again why that ratty old thing was so important.

He didn't think the goons waiting for him would still be around, but they were ready anyway. Erin had grabbed a back-up gun from the house before they left. Her colleagues had confiscated her Glock-19 for evidence. The back-up was equally potent, a Model 19 Smith & Wesson .357 revolver. She told Scott it was her father's gun.

The door opened easily, and they stepped inside. Stiletto stood and examined the room for a few moments, Erin standing behind him with her right hand in her purse where she'd put her gun. There was no sign of a disturbance. The hotel room remained as neat and tidy as Scott had left it. The maid service had come and gone, and the bed was neatly made.

"All right?" she said.

"Maybe they didn't show up after all." Stiletto shut the door.

"How would they have gotten in?"

Stiletto scoffed. "Plenty of ways to defeat an electronic lock. Worst thing hotels ever did for guest security was switch over to those."

He took off his own jacket and draped it across the back of a chair by the window.

"Can you open the drapes?"

"No."

She didn't ask again.

He said, "You're probably ready for some rest, right?"

"It's getting tough to keep my eyes open, yeah."

"Go ahead and lay down. I'll doze off in the chair."

She shrugged off her jean jacket and stretched out on the bed with a sigh. "Turn off the light."

"You're welcome," he said, switching off the lamps before easing into the reclining chair. She started snoring before he fell asleep.

Stiletto awoke with a start as Erin shook his shoulder.

"What time is it?" he asked, wiping his eyes.

"After two, and I'm starving," she said.

A sliver of sunlight broke through the crack between the drapes. It was probably another beautiful day.

He told her where to find the room service menu. She asked again about the drapes, but when he told her they needed to stay closed, she said whatever and dropped the subject. Scott noticed the jean jacket on the bed, inside out, and a name written in black marker across the collar that wasn't Erin's. The ink had faded in a few spots, but the writing was clear enough: Tina.

"What do you want?" she asked.

"A burger is fine." Stiletto rose from the recliner and went into the bathroom. When he came out, she told him the food would be up in a half-hour.

She sat at the table while he took his spot on the recliner. "Sleep okay?" he said.

"Bad dreams."

"Tell me about it."

"Why don't you," she said, "instead tell me what you've learned." She grabbed the notepad and a pen from the corner desk.

Stiletto began his story with his acquisition of Shelly's diary, which he brought out of hiding to show Erin.

CHAPTER NINETEEN

"I didn't know this existed," Detective Erin Keene said as she paged through the diary.

Stiletto sat on the opposite side of the table and watched Erin while she read.

"Usual girl stuff," she said.

"Uh-huh."

"It looks like a good chronicle of her time in Twin Falls."

Stiletto nodded.

Erin turned more pages, scanning the words, then closed the book. "Is that it?"

"You missed the best part."

"Which?"

"The back."

She turned to the last page and frowned at the coded phrases. "Is this a joke?"

"It's a code," he said. "She interviewed for a job at a night club and took a liking to the owner's son." He told her about Roger and Peter Ivy and his visit with them, leaving out the part where he waved around a pistol to keep them from calling the police. She probably wouldn't have appreciated that detail.

"She told him a lot, about wanting to leave Chad, about how she didn't like some friends he had."

"Friends you met at the Shipwreck?"

Stiletto nodded.

"Peter Ivy and Penny and Vicki gave me the name 'Damien.' He's apparently the ringleader. They didn't have any other names."

"Hopefully they'll show up at the Shipwreck again."

She reacted with disgust, closing the diary and pushing it in his direction.

"I'm a by-the-book cop, Scott," she said. "If you think I'm going to engage in any vigilante action—"

"I don't see that you have any choice, Detective," Stiletto said. "The cops last night were only interested in getting those punks clear of the scene and putting me away. Nobody tried to sort out what happened. Even the bartender lied. Whoever is in charge of this town, whoever runs the syndicate and calls the shots, has this place so wired it's going to take somebody like me to knock down his house."

She stared at him a moment.

"Come on," he said. "Don't tell me you and some of the other honest cops in Twin Falls haven't wished for something like this to happen."

"It might have crossed our minds," she said, "but we aren't going to beat the bad guys by becoming bad guys."

"Yet you didn't hesitate to point me in the direction of witnesses you said refused to talk to you."

"Shelly's murder is a cold case. Maybe you shaking things up will lead us to her killer. That doesn't mean I'm pretending I'm Charles Bronson."

"They've tried to murder you, Erin. They did that because I'm getting too close, and you allied yourself with me by getting me out of jail. By the way, was that by the book?"

"Technically."

Stiletto laughed. "Obviously you're not afraid to bend the rules when you're basically right or when it's convenient, but I don't buy the rest of it. Somewhere deep down you want to turn over tables to get to the bottom of this case, no matter what you have to do. Right?"

She sank into the chair. "And others," she muttered.

"Whose name is on your jacket?"

She blinked. "What?"

"The faded name on the collar. 'Tina.' Who is that?"

"You mean, who was Tina."

"Sure."

"She's the reason I became a cop," Erin Keene said. The answer stunned Stiletto to silence. He waited.

"Tina Lawson was my best friend growing up," she said. "When we were in high school, the football quarterback raped her. The cops didn't believe her because he had an alibi. He walked."

"They didn't do a test? Get DNA?"

"The lab said the DNA was inconclusive and partially contaminated. Cops got a warrant for a new test, but it came back negative, not a match."

Stiletto listened some more.

"Tina killed herself a few years later," Erin said. "I was in college when it happened. I was going to be an architect, but after she died, I took the police test and went to the academy. And I kept her jacket."

"Was this quarterback somebody special?"

"A rich man's kid."

"Aren't they always? What was his name?"

She didn't hesitate. "Kurt Swanberg."

"Where is he now?"

"Right here in Twin Falls," she said. "He went away and made his own fortune, then came back after his father died to live on a big piece of property south of the city and treat Twin Falls like his personal kingdom. And there's nothing I can do about it."

There was a knock on the door. Stiletto and Erin froze.

From the other side, somebody called, "Room service."

Erin had ordered two hamburgers, a BBQ bacon burger for herself, dripping with sauce and melted cheese, and a regular for Stiletto, to which he added plenty of mustard.

"Is Swanberg connected to the syndicate?" Stiletto said.

"I wish," she said between bites. "But no."

"What about Boskowictz?"

"That snake," she said. "He's been on the take since he left the academy, if not before. He's caused a lot of problems, despite still being in uniform and on traffic duty."

They ate quietly for a while. Stiletto thought about putting some music on but decided not to.

"Who's in charge of the syndicate?" Stiletto said.

"You really think it goes that high?"

"Somebody is going to great lengths to cover for that gang I tangled with."

She swallowed a bite. "The big boss of Twin Falls, if that doesn't make you laugh, is Ben Giordana."

"Where does he hang out?"

"Why don't you ask his daughter?"

"Who's that?"

"Your friend Chloe."

Stiletto's pulse quickened, and he stared across the table at the detective. She didn't break eye contact. She wasn't lying.

CHAPTER TWENTY

"Is she involved?"

"Oh, no," Erin said. "They've been on the outs for a few years now. They don't talk to each other. He'll drop in at her apartment for a surprise visit now and then, but they never talk long."

Stiletto ate a French fry and sipped his drink. "What's the story?"

"Nobody really knows, but the best guess is that Chloe found out what her father actually does for a living and didn't want any part of it. To buy that diner, she had some help from the previous owner, but after that, especially after her husband ran out on her, she pulled that place together on her own."

"Doesn't surprise me."

"Word is," Erin said, "that Ben is trying to find his granddaughter as a peace offering. He hasn't had any luck yet."

"You mean his people haven't."

She laughed. "Right. The big boss never does anything on his own."

Stiletto found his appetite again. They ate some more.

"Ben's getting close to seventy," Erin said. "He needs Chloe. He doesn't want to die alone."

"Does Boskowictz work for Ben?"

"He did for a long time, but there are rumors that even Sergeant Boz isn't as enamored with Ben Giordana as he used to be."

"Why?"

"Nobody knows. All we know is that they have arguments now and then, and that's not how a subordinate speaks to his boss."

Stiletto ate a few bites and thought about the aging gangster who wanted his daughter back, so he didn't die by himself. Stiletto hated the idea of sympathizing with Mafiosi, but he had to admit he understood the old man's feelings on that score.

He faced the same fate himself if he didn't reconnect with Felicia or find another woman with whom to spend the rest of his years. But how do you settle down when all you know how to do is fight somebody else's war?

"Did you learn anything during the fight at the bar?" Erin said. "We can look up anybody named Damien in town since I don't think it's a common name, but that's a lot of time and effort for not a quick return. And then I'd have trouble explaining why we needed to talk to them."

"What about that name I overheard the other night?

Doug Armstrong. Did you look him up, by chance?"

"Investment banker," Erin said. "He runs his own firm and does a lot of civic stuff. Charity events, things like that."

"Is he dirty?"

"No record that I know of."

"Can you find out?"

"We're not allowed to look up people because we think they might be bad guys, Scott. One of my colleagues once earned a two-week suspension because she moved into a new house and ran the license plates of everybody in her cul-de-sac to see if her neighbors were crooks. That's a no-no. This is America, remember?"

"You'd be surprised what happens in America, Erin."

"What are your plans, then?"

"I'm going to find Armstrong and learn who his kid is, and then I'm going to make him talk."

"Don't break any laws."

"No promises."

"Don't tell me if you've broken any laws."

"That I can manage."

She smiled.

"What about you?"

"I think I'll see if the hotel has any vacancies. It's probably a good idea not to stay home for a while."

Stiletto didn't argue.

The cherry-red Mercedes SLS AMG thundered through the entrance of the underground garage of a downtown building.

Vincent Six steered the sleek gull-wing coupe into a reserved parking slot near the elevator. The garage was full of cars—none as fancy as the SLS—but Six paid no attention. The driver's door swung out and up, resembling a small wing after it had reached full height. He swung his legs out of the vehicle and stood, using two hands to lower the gull-wing door to the closed position. The car chirped as the doors locked and the alarm activated, and by then Six was waiting for the elevator.

"Six" was not his real surname. He had been born Vincent Coburn in Tacoma, Washington more years ago than he cared to recall. He'd earned the nickname "Six" after whacking that number of guys in one hit despite facing more guns than he carried and walking out without a scratch.

The elevator doors rumbled open. The elevator car had faux-aluminum paneling on the walls and Six used a key to access the penthouse. The doors rumbled shut, and the elevator started upward. The motor was quiet, so Six only had a slight sense of motion to tell him the car was ascending.

He was home early. He had been unable to accomplish the mission of locating the chief's granddaughter, but her trail hadn't gone cold. He had enough leads to pick up her trail again when the current crisis was over.

Six and Ben Giordana had worked together for several decades, and Six, while at the moment having no information on the problem the chief needed him to solve, cleared his mind of the last few weeks and focused on the coming tasks.

Because nobody messed with his pal, not without paying the consequences. Vincent "Six" Coburn specialized in consequences.

CHAPTER TWENTY-ONE

Six wore a gray suit that had been tailored to fit his stout frame, complete with black steel-toed shoes that were always spit-shined to the point where he could see his reflection if he looked hard enough.

He wore his hair close-cropped and didn't color it despite patches of white. He'd earned the white. The white matched the lines on his face. He wore the evidence that he'd been through the fire and emerged unscathed. It was an important message to communicate, even to allies. Everyone needed to know that Vince Six was a man to fear. A man you didn't want to cross.

The elevator doors slid open, revealing a small welcome area that was the exact opposite. Two goons with muscles stretching the fabric of their suits stood on either side of a double door. The doorframe was white. The walls were beige and bare. White tile instead of carpeting. It was as antiseptic as a hospital.

Six identified himself and submitted to a pat-down. Six

carried no guns, and the luggage from his trip remained in the trunk of the car downstairs. His hardware was packed with his clothes and other necessities.

The goon who did not pat Six down radioed somebody beyond the white-trimmed door and told Six to wait. Six stood quietly. These men did not know him. He did not know them. He wasn't the "do you know who I am?" type, especially in the boss's parlor.

The door opened, and another goon escorted Six into the inner sanctum.

Ben Giordana's penthouse apartment was decorated in nothing but the best, but the effect was lost on Six. He'd seen it all too many times to be impressed. The boss was out on the balcony and Six's escort led him across the main room, with its soft carpet and sunken center where two couches and a coffee table sat.

"Welcome home, Vince," Giordana said. He dismissed the escort and gestured to a tray between his chair and an empty one. "Have a seat. Help yourself."

Six took the empty chair. He wiped his forehead with the back of his left hand.

"Didn't dress for the weather, did you?" Giordana asked.

"It's a little hot."

"Ninety-one."

"Sounds about right." Six filled a glass with ice, a little bourbon, and a shot of seltzer. "Still a nice view, though."

Giordana's penthouse overlooked a portion of the

winding valley known as Snake River, with a little of Highway 93 running north-south across the gap.

"They're still alive," Giordana said.

Six swallowed some of his drink. "What do we do next?"

"I'm not sure."

"The turkey is going to want answers."

"And he'll send Boscowictz to ask the questions. I'm aware." Giordana held a half-empty glass in his left hand, letting it dangle a little as his forearm lay on the armrest of the chair. "The turkey is the worst thing that ever happened to this place. We had a good thing going until he came back."

"You never told me why he has such a hold on you."

"You're right."

Giordana sipped his drink.

Six took a breath and admired the view. For whatever reason, the boss jumped when the turkey south of town told him to, and Six had no idea why. Giordana had never volunteered the information and there were no rumors to sort into a coherent narrative. Someday he'd find out.

"You want to give me some background, boss? What led up to you sending two shooters against a cop and this other dude?"

Giordana updated Six on the happenings of the last few days. Six listened carefully.

"You want my opinion?" Six said.

"That's why I brought you back here, Vince."

"Get this stranger on our side. Let's bring him in, tell him what really happened, and have him settle a bunch of problems at once."

"That puts my daughter at risk."

"We're going to need to risk several things to get the turkey off our backs."

"I'm not risking Chloe."

"Yes, sir."

"How close did you come to finding my granddaughter?"

"Close enough that the trail will be easy to pick up once I'm done here. What exactly am I doing here, Ben?"

Giordana only downed more of his drink. His eyes remained on the Snake River in the distance, and the sudden realization that the boss was mentally immobilized and unable to see his way out of the current crisis told Six all he needed to know.

"Why don't you leave it to me, huh?" Six said.

"Nothing that hurts Chloe."

Six powered down the rest of the bourdon. The ice clinked as he set the glass down.

"Never, Ben." Six rose and buttoned his suit jacket.

"Get out of this heat, for heaven's sake," Giordana told him. He rose and shook Six's hand. Six looked at the old man's eyes. Instead of fear, Vince saw relief.

Six was escorted out of the penthouse by the same attendant and bid farewell to the guards as the elevator doors slid shut once again.

The boss needed him big time and no mistake. Six cracked his knuckles as he started considering ideas. He wanted to see the stranger everybody was getting so worked up about, but first, he wanted to visit the Idaho State Correctional Institution two hours away in Boise.

The issue with the turkey had gone on long enough, and this time, it posed a serious threat. The situation was spiraling out of control. Six needed to sort out that problem, and if the boss wasn't going to tell him, he knew somebody who might know. Somebody locked away in a cell.

Well, not right away. He had his own needs to attend to, like getting unpacked, taking a shower, and finding a way to feel normal again after weeks on the road.

He'd start his mission first thing in the morning.

CHAPTER TWENTY-TWO

"Up to your old tricks, Six?"

"If I hadn't told them I was your new lawyer, they wouldn't have given us this private room," Six said. "Plus, I got this new suit and briefcase to sell the part."

"I'm sure they bought it. Did your shoes set off the metal detector?"

"These don't have steel toes."

"Ha."

"Sit down. We need to talk."

"About what?"

"The boss is in trouble, and I need your help. Sit down. I'm not telling you again."

"What happens if I don't?"

Vince Six quietly regarded the man behind him. Sam Patten had put on a little weight since his fifteen-year sentence began, and the orange jumpsuit looked too small and hung oddly on his frame. Most of his hair was gone now, but he hadn't grown a beard to cover the sharp jawline that had always been a distinguishing feature and a turn-on for the ladies. His wrists were shackled in front of him, but his feet were free.

"Sam," Six said, "I know we've had our differences, but we need to put them aside. Ben is in trouble. I don't know anybody else who can help me."

Patten laughed. "I bet that was hard to say."

"Not when my friend needs help, it wasn't. You gonna sit, or do I break your legs?"

"Same old Six," Patten said. He pulled the small chair out from the table in the center of the cold room and sat down.

A prison guard stood outside the thick steel doorway, ready for "the lawyer" to announce the end of the meeting.

Six set the briefcase on the table.

"Anything in there?"

"Enough to fool the x-ray scan."

Patten rested his rests on the metal table. The cuffs clanged. "What's going on?"

Six told Patten why he had been recalled home and the issues surrounding the new developments in the Shelly Pierce case.

"The turkey," Six said. "What does he have on Ben?"

Patten laughed. "I'm supposed to know?"

"Stop it, Sam. You know everything."

"You know who the turkey is, right?"

"Kurt Swanberg, yeah. I know he showed up a decade ago, and Ben hasn't been the same since."

"Swanberg has something on Ben. Something big enough to make Ben do what he says. Something big enough to make Swanberg the de facto boss of the outfit in Twin Falls, and nobody in New York City knows what the real score is here."

"What is that something?"

"I appreciate you think I know everything, Six, but that's one thing I never learned. I have no idea what Ben is being blackmailed with. And make no mistake, Swanberg is blackmailing Ben."

"What do you suggest I do, then? We have to get Ben out from under this."

"Because of his kid?"

"Especially his kid."

"Still have a soft spot for her?" Patten grinned.

Six pressed his lips together tightly.

He balled a fist, but kept it under the table and watched Sam Patten grin like he'd won some sort of victory.

Six's "soft spot" for Chloe Giordana wasn't anything lecherous or romantic. It wasn't anything other than one man caring about another man's daughter as his own, because had life turned out better for Six and his now-dead wife and daughter, his own child and Chloe might have been friends.

"I'm trying to bury the hatchet, Sam," Vince Six said. "But if you'd like, I can see that you're severely injured in your cell or on the yard. You'll never see it coming."

Patten's grin vanished. "Hey, I didn't mean nothing."

"I'm sure. How do I go about solving the boss's problems?"

"You need to dig into Swanberg's background. You can start with somebody in Twin Falls who might be willing to share some of Swanberg's dirty laundry. You know, if you ask nicely."

"Who?"

"Kevin Osslo. I'm not sure where he lives now, but I know he's still in town."

Vince Six scraped back the metal chair and grabbed his briefcase. He glared at Patten as he went to the door and pounded on it, announcing to the guard who stepped inside that he was done speaking to his client.

Six felt Patten's eyes on his back as he walked out, but he didn't say good-bye.

The drive back to Twin Falls took two hours, and Vince Six sat behind the wheel with a lot on his mind.

He knew only the basics about Kurt Swanberg.

Native of Twin Falls. The son of a wealthy family. High school football star, but not good enough for the full-ride scholarship he'd wanted. He'd instead used his father's generous college graduation gift to get him to California, where he started a high-tech company and revolutionized computer anti-virus protection. After becoming a multi-millionaire, he returned to Twin Falls and lived like a hermit. He excelled at keeping out of the public eye. He had a son of his own named Damien, who was at least in his mid-twenties and was divorced. That was the sum of Six's knowledge about Kurt Swanberg. If the man had a sketchy background that had put him in contact with people like Ben Giordana, it was a surprise to Six. It wasn't easy to remain unknown in the underworld, and if Swanberg had figured out a way to stay anonymous, Six wanted to know his secret.

Kevin Osslo would have answers to Six's growing list of questions.

He drove on.

CHAPTER TWENTY-THREE

Vince Six parked his Chrysler a few doors down from Kevin Osslo's home and approached on foot.

Mid-afternoon, the neighborhood was quiet. A truck passed. A dog barked. All was stable, but Six's danger scan didn't cease. He was used to always checking for threats, even in his own home, and it was a hard habit to break. Six knew the day he broke the habit might be his last.

His shoes tapped quietly on the sidewalk, and he paused at Osslo's mailbox. The yard in front of the house was well-kept, the hedge between the sidewalk and grass trimmed to perfection. The driveway was empty, but there was an oil spot on the right-hand side. The lower half of the garage door looked like it had sustained impact damage sometime in the past.

Six knew Osslo from the old days. He had operated a casino for the Giordana organization, one that was supposed to be run by the Fort Hall Indian Reservation. The fact that Fort Hall was far from Twin Falls County was brushed over via payoffs to state officials. Osslo had left the organization after health issues had interfered with his work. Six wasn't sure what he knew, but Patten had said he knew something. Vince was hoped Patten's loyalty to Giordana and ignoring any animosity he had toward Six had made him tell the truth.

Six moved on from the mailbox and up the driveway. He didn't know what shape Osslo was in or if he was friendly toward visitors from the old outfit, so he approached cautiously. Smiling at the No Solicitors sign near the door, he knocked.

"Who's there?" a voice on the other side of the door called. The man sounded older. Osslo was older than Six by about six years, so he more than likely had the right person.

"Vince Coburn."

"Who?"

"Vince Six," the enforcer said, raising his voice.

A chain rattled, a deadbolt snapped back, and the door opened a few inches. Half a face showed in the gap. Osslo wore glasses and extra flesh dangled below his chin.

"What is it?"

"I need your help."

"You or Ben?"

"Both of us."

"What's going on?"

"Ben's in trouble."

"So?"

"Because of Swanberg."

Osslo's face softened a little. "He up to his old tricks?"

"I need to talk to you, Kevin. I need to know what Swanberg has on Ben so I can take the heat off."

"Permanently?"

"By whatever means necessary."

Osslo opened the door all the way. "Let's talk, then. You feel like a beer?"

Six stepped through the door and into the cool house. "A beer would be great."

They sat in the kitchen at a small, very clean table in a corner partially surrounded by windows. The backyard looked as immaculate as the front.

"You do all this yard work yourself?"

Osslo placed a bottle of beer in front of Six. "Most of it. I have help with the big stuff. I'm not as chipper as I used to be."

Osslo eased into a chair opposite Six. He drank from his bottle, and Six followed suit.

Osslo set the bottle down. "What's on your mind?"

"Tell me about Swanberg."

Osslo laughed. "Ben not telling you?"

"No."

"Does he know you're here?"

Six shook his head. "No."

"He's shy about it."

"Sounds like an understatement."

Osslo paused for a minute to collect his thoughts. Six didn't prompt him. There were no sounds in the house.

"You know about Swanberg's business?"

"Computers, anti-virus software, yeah."

"He bribed his way to the top, you know. He did a lot of his own work, sure, but if he found a competitor or a private party who had more on the ball than he did, he bought their stuff, one way or another. Threats, intimidation, whatever it took. He paid for those things in cash, so there wasn't a record. If you go asking around California, you'll hear some stories, but there isn't any hard evidence."

Six nodded. "Did anybody try to stop him?"

"A group of Silicon Valley people got together and tried to raise a stink, but Swanberg had connections. Local mob guys, stuff like that. He used them to shut those guys up and make them go away. Threats to their family, that sort of thing."

"Uh-huh."

"That's when Swanberg started using blackmail to keep everybody quiet. If he could find something to use against another guy, he didn't hesitate."

Six nodded.

"Swanberg made his millions, cashed it all in, and came back to Twin Falls with that kid of his."

"What happened to his wife?"

Osslo shrugged. "Nobody knows. She disappeared before they returned. It's an open case in California, but nobody has ever come forward or even filed a formal missing person report."

"Interesting."

"Swanberg is sitting pretty at that property of his and then he gets Ben under his thumb."

"How?"

"Not sure."

"What do you mean, not sure? I was told you knew."

"Who told you?"

"Sam Patten."

Osslo laughed. "That punk. He doesn't know what he doesn't know. He assumed a lot of things, and he was wrong about most of them."

"Kevin, how am I supposed to help Ben if I don't know what Swanberg has on him? Somebody's gotta know."

Osslo swallowed some beer. "I hear ya. You need to talk to one of Swanberg's guys."

"Are you kidding me?"

"Nope. Tim Dell is the guy's name. He runs—"

"The Tom Tom Club, I know. Is he really the owner, or does Swanberg have an interest?"

"Swanberg has an interest, yeah."

"And Dell will talk?"

Osslo laughed. "He'll blow you off. You'll need to apply a little pressure."

Six pushed the half-full beer away. He appreciated Os-slo's information, but he hadn't come for a background lesson. Reaching one's goal was never easy, but dealing with a minor thug like Tim Dell shouldn't be too hard.

"Are you upset with me, Vince?"

"I'm upset with Patten."

"You should be."

Six scooted back his chair and stood up. Osslo did not rise.

"I'm sorry I couldn't give you more," the old man said. "I tried to find the answers, but Ben was never any help."

"I'll find them."

Osslo rose and escorted Six to the door.

Vince Six drove away in the Chrysler, trying to decide the best time to visit the Tom Tom Club and see a man named Tim Dell.

CHAPTER TWENTY-FOUR

Stiletto had spent the last two days watching Douglas Armstrong and noting his movements. It wasn't a new exercise. For his entire career, whether he was planning to assassinate a target or take out a terror suspect, a period of study was required before making any moves. You needed to know when your subject left his home, which route he took to work, whatever his routine was. If you only watched for three days and your target played tennis Monday, Tuesday, and Wednesday, and you planned the hit for Thursday night, only to discover too late that's the only night he didn't play tennis, the game was over. You had to watch your target long enough to know where he might be at every moment of the day or evening. In this case, Armstrong kept to the same routine, and Stiletto's only regret was that he had to make a move after only two days.

He began by looking up Doug Armstrong's company on the internet, noting the company address and printing a photo of the man for reference. A Dissenter search revealed a few newspaper stories about Armstrong, his profitable investment firm, and his philanthropic efforts in Twin Falls that mentioned his family and other pertinent details. His son, Joe, was an only child and had so far not enrolled in college, despite graduating high school with high marks.

Doug left his office for lunch every day at 12:15 and went to the same sit-down restaurant for his meal. Scott ate there too on the second day, and the staff knew Armstrong well. The owner came out to speak to him about some investment ideas and made an appointment to see Armstrong at his office the next week.

The father's activities did not intersect with the son. Joe did not live with his parents, but Stiletto knew it was only a matter of time before he showed up at home, and his patience was thankfully rewarded on the second night. Joe pulled up to the house in a tricked-out Shelby Cobra replica, the 427-engine rumbling loudly, the rumble increased by fat side pipes along either side of the roadster. Stiletto watched from the opposite cul-de-sac.

A few hours later, Joe Armstrong jumped back into his Cobra and powered away. Stiletto had to hustle to keep up. His four-cylinder rental was no match for the Windsor V8 under the Cobra's scooped hood.

Thickening evening traffic helped, and soon Stiletto figured out where they were heading.

Back to the Shipwreck Bar.

That was what Stiletto had been counting on. He

wanted to see inside the second-floor loft. He wanted to know what the gang was up to, to see if he could find any evidence tying them to Chad and Shelly's murder. Failing that, he'd revert to grabbing one or two and working them over until they spilled the beans.

To facilitate his entry into the loft, he'd brought along a set of lock picks. They weighed down the left side of his coat where his gun would normally ride. The Colt .45 remained at the hotel. He did not want to get caught carrying a gun without a license. He didn't think Detective Erin Keene could get him out of trouble like that as easily as she'd sprung him from jail.

Stiletto pulled over near the same parking spot he'd used on his last visit as the Cobra turned into the side parking lot of the bar. Stiletto sat in the car for a moment. He'd be recognized if he stepped back into the bar, and he had no disguise. He left the rental anyway. Walking along the side of the road, noting the shadows of the buildings to his left, he cut through the cluttered side yard of a car repair shop and stopped at a fence. He used a stack of old tires for cover as he observed the rear of the Shipwreck Bar and the side lot.

There were fewer cars than there had been the other night. Smokers near the side door, as usual. This time, Stiletto had a good look at the back wall and saw a door there too. Two large dumpsters sat a few feet from the rear door, but the set of steps leading to the second-floor loft held Stiletto's attention more than anything. Joe Armstrong had parked his Cobra near the back wall.

The security lights along the back shone brightly. They hadn't been there the other night. Had they needed to change the bulbs or had the view been blocked by cars? Stiletto couldn't remember getting a glance at the rear, so it was certainly possible. Those steps greatly helped his cause.

The lights were on upstairs. Stiletto stood still, letting the shadows swallow him whole. All he had to do was wait. Why had the gang returned to the bar after the fight? Either the gang had nowhere else to go for their clubhouse, or they thought it didn't matter because they were so well protected and Scott was still in jail. Such assumptions had doomed many of Stiletto's previous adversaries.

He wondered how Joe, Damien, and the other two were holding up after the pounding he'd given them. The memory made him smile. Nothing satisfied Stiletto more than giving a beating to somebody who deserved one.

The smokers ground out their butts and went back into the bar. The night sounds remained steady. Cars drove by. No headlamps flashed over Scott's position. People walked by, too busy talking to notice him hiding.

Stiletto shifted now and then as the minutes ticked by. After seemingly forever, the door to the second-story loft finally opened, and three men started down the steps. The last one to leave turned off the lights, pulled the door shut, and locked it. Stiletto noted that he did not turn a dead-bolt, so the loft was only protected by a simple knob lock.

Joe Armstrong slid behind the wheel of the Cobra and departed with the sound of fury coming out of the exhausts.

The other two climbed into a more conservative Accord.

None of the trio walked quickly. Damien had a bandage on his neck and marks on his face. The third man Scott hadn't been able to get a good look at. They were walking wounded. Whatever they were doing, whatever plans they were making in the loft, the schedule did not allow for recuperation time.

The sound of the Cobra replica faded into the night. The Accord blended into traffic. More smokers exited to have their puffs and chat. When the group returned to the bar, Stiletto left the car repair lot and circled the fence. He dashed for the rear steps and hoped nobody emerged from the back to take out the trash.

CHAPTER TWENTY-FIVE

Scott opened the leather pouch containing the lock picks and went to work on the knob. It didn't take long. He inserted the guide pick through the keyhole, pushing it until it stopped. The second pick he inserted over the top of the first. The second pick was the one that moved the tumblers and allowed him to twist the doorknob. The door opened a few inches. Stiletto pulled out the picks and shut the door, returning the gear to the pouch and his jacket. He used a mini Maglite to scan the loft.

It was narrow and long instead of wide, running the length of the bar below.

The gang did not use the place for sleeping. There was no bed, only a large television with a circular couch in front at the far end. Elsewhere were tables and chairs and assorted clutter. It was a bachelor hangout. A small refrigerator held beer. One table showed the remains of a Cheetos. Scott converged on the other table when his Maglite showed a map spread across the top. He'd almost passed by, thinking it was a tablecloth, but took a second look when he realized a tablecloth would be nowhere near a hideout like this.

He quickly shone the flash on the map, then removed his cell phone to take pictures. With the volume off, the phone made no sound as he snapped the pictures. As he took the shots, he processed what he was looking at. The crew couldn't have been more obvious, but many pieces of the puzzle were missing.

The map was dotted with notes about when "the courier" was departing. A section of northbound 93 leading out of Twin Falls for Falls City had an X off to the side, with the initials PONR next to it. Scott knew PONR was a pilot's term: Point of No Return. It was usually the moment during a flight where pilots would not have enough fuel to turn back to where they'd taken off from and had to complete the flight plan. If an aircraft had an issue during this time, such a moment had its complications.

Which of the wild bunch was a pilot?

Stiletto filed the question for later.

He took another picture while holding the phone above the map to get the whole thing for a nice zoom-in later. Turning off the mini Maglite, he pocketed the flash and made his exit. He was able to get away quickly. There weren't any smokers hanging out in the parking lot.

Joe Armstrong never noticed he was being followed.

Joe and his pals lived with the idea that they were untouchable, thanks to Damien's father, his father, and all the city officials and cops both men had on their payroll. It wasn't a notion from which they could be shaken. They had free rein. The other night when that dude had attacked them in front of the Shipwreck was a perfect example. The cops, upon hearing Joe say his father's name, ushered them out as if they'd never been there at all.

Except for Eric. Eric Foster was still in the hospital, thanks to the concussion received during the fight. The son of a bitch who'd hassled them had struck Eric in the head with a knee.

The mystery man was the only problem they'd encountered thus far, but Joe wasn't the only one who wondered who the man was, or why he'd picked that moment to introduce himself. He had an idea, of course. Damien did, too. But all they had was an idea, nothing to go on that was solid. Until they had information, there was still work to do.

His replica Cobra thundered toward the Shipwreck, and he didn't brake as he swung the stubby front end onto the parking lot's pavement and stopped in front of the rear steps of the bar. The smokers outside glanced his way. The woman didn't look long. The guys' gazes remained on the car as Armstrong hopped out and went up to the loft.

Damien Swanberg looked up as Joe entered. Damien was bruised and had a bandage on his neck where the bastard had ground out a cigar, but otherwise, he was firing all eight cylinders. His bony jaw remained his most prominent feature, along with his muscular bulk.

Damien Swanberg was the ringleader of their gang, and he was the typical dark-and-brooding type with thick black hair and a skinny but wiry body. He was not only the ringleader but also the mastermind. Every job they'd pulled had been scouted and set up by Damien. The four of them did the planning since every guy had a role that needed to be played to perfection, but the genesis of every score came from Damien's brain.

Teddy Stone was shorter than Damien, thicker all around, and good with a gun. Eric was their other shooter, and both spent a lot of time at the shooting range doing target practice.

Joe Armstrong was the team's driver. There wasn't anything on four wheels the wiry man couldn't manipulate to his every whim.

"Shut the door," Damien said.

Joe was about to argue when he turned and looked. The door hadn't closed all the way when he'd given it a push upon entering. He closed it all the way.

"We've worked out where we're going to hit the courier," Damien said.

The details of the heist weren't Joe's concern. His

concern was where he was driving and when the others wanted to make the score. He listened carefully as Damien explained the route. He had the car prepped. He'd found an old Ford Crown Vic that was perfect for the role. The engine was properly juiced for more power, and the suspension worked over for better stability and cornering. All he needed was the gun crew, Damien and Teddy.

Too bad Eric was still in the hospital.

Joe listened anyway as Damien gave the rundown.

"The courier leaves the mall store at 1:30 every Thursday. He keeps the stones in a strongbox locked inside another strongbox, set on his passenger seat. Inside the first strongbox are smaller steel boxes containing the number of stones each store gets. Three stores, three boxes apiece, we're looking at nine boxes of stones."

"How much?" Armstrong said.

"Maybe a million if we get lucky. At the least, half a million. Do a four-way split, that's $125,000 for your time, boys."

"We still splitting four ways even though Eric isn't with us?" Ted Stone asked.

"Of course," Damien said with a sharp look at Ted. "You follow the guy, do a fender-bender, stick a gun in his face, and take the stones. Easy."

Armstrong and Stone nodded.

"No killing," Damien said. "The guy isn't armed. He won't play hero. But if he gives you any lip, clock 'im."

"No killing," Stone said.

Damien said, "That's it, guys."

"When do we leave?" Armstrong asked.

"Tomorrow. Noon sharp. We need to catch the courier when he leaves at 1:30."

Joe Armstrong couldn't wait.

CHAPTER TWENTY-SIX

The only thing that concerned Joe Armstrong as he and Damien and Ted Stone sat in the back of a bar that wasn't the Shipwreck was why the diamond shipment wasn't being escorted out of town via armored van.

"With that kind of haul," he said, "you'd think they'd move it the same way they move their cash."

It was easy to talk because of the music and the crowd. The air was thick with the smell of sweat from the bodies on the dance floor.

Damien considered the question while he ate a loaded potato skin and washed it down with beer.

"My inside guy says it's actually a minor shipment compared to the regular armored runs and it costs more to move using the armored truck. With one courier they can put some fat insurance on the load, dude can make his stops, and nobody cries too hard if the ice gets taken as long as the courier isn't hurt."

"Why not hurt him?" Ted Stone said. "We're covered."

"Keep cool," Damien said. "I don't know what's going on with mystery man from the other night. Until we know more, no rough stuff."

Ted Stone shrugged. "Sure."

"That dude still in jail?" Armstrong asked.

"Naw, he's out."

"What?"

"They let him out because there were no witnesses or some crap. We were too busy getting patched up at the hospital to worry about that."

"But he's out there. He's looking for us. We don't know why."

Damien swallowed more beer. "Uh-huh."

"I don't like that."

"I don't either, but it probably helps us."

"How?"

"He comes at us again, we'll be ready."

Armstrong scoffed.

"It's about that girl," Ted Stone said. "What's-'er-ass. The one Chad was banging."

"Uh-huh," Damien said. He ate another potato skin.

Armstrong pushed his beer away. He didn't want any more; the potato skins looked gross. His head hurt from the loud music. Knowing Mystery Man was out there, most likely looking for payback over what they had done to Chad and his girlfriend, suddenly took away his ability or desire to party.

"You two calm down," Damien said. "My father is looking for him. We don't have to worry."

Armstrong didn't acknowledge the remark.

The diamond courier took off from Jewelry Central in the Magic Valley Mall. Damien, in the passenger seat of the souped-up Ford, gritted his teeth at the numberless potholes and rough patches in the crowded street as the gang followed. The freeway would be a better ride.

Pedestrians were everywhere, ignoring traffic signals and slowing traffic down. Construction crews blocked lanes, and delivery trucks double-parked. When the delays became too infuriating, Damien looked at the mountains in the distance. The nice thing about Twin Falls was he could always look at the mountains and let his mind wander to places other than noisy construction zones.

Armstrong drove, with Ted Stone in the back seat. All wore dark windbreakers and gloves. Guns under their armpits, use-'em-and-lose-'em Rossi .38s. Nothing fancy needed for a job like this.

Armstrong had no problem keeping up, especially once the courier reached the onramp to northbound 93 for Falls City. The low growl from under the hood of the tricked-out Crown Vic sounded better than music to Armstrong. He took a deep breath and tried to settle down.

The freeway began to curve to the right, Armstrong taking it easy. One of the cars in front of the courier's

Chevy took an exit, leaving only one car between the Ford and the courier's vehicle. The curve drifted left. They crossed the Perrine Memorial Bridge, and it was hard not to look at the winding Snake River below. Open country, all tan and hazy, mountains in the distance, offered the opportunity for serene reflection, but contemplation of his place of the world wasn't on Armstrong's mind as he stayed with the Chevy.

"Do or die at the 84 interchange, Joe," Damien said. "Gotta get closer."

Traffic in the middle lane offered no openings for Armstrong. He cursed under his breath, but then switched lanes when a SUV moved into the left lane. He stepped on the gas and let off the throttle as soon as he reached the courier's blind spot.

"Go, Joe!" Damien shouted.

The Ford's engine growled, the car shot forward, and metal crunched as the Ford's bumper slammed into the back of the courier car.

The three crooks were jolted against their seatbelts.

The courier started moving to the shoulder. Armstrong followed.

Before Armstrong had stopped, Damien and Stone sprang out of the Ford and rushed to the courier's car.

The courier had his door open, his feet just touching the pavement, when Damien shoved him back into the seat and jammed the .38 in his face.

The courier went white. "Hey, wait!"

"Shut up."

Glass shattered as Ted Stone pounded the passenger door's window with the butt of his gun. He reached in and unlocked the door.

"Don't kill me! Take it all but don't kill me!"

"Shut up!" Damien said. Held his .38 steady, beads of sweat on his forehead, breathing slow and deep. He didn't blink as he stared into the courier's wide eyes.

Ted Stone put his gun away, then grabbed the handles of the strongbox and tried to lift it out, but it wouldn't budge. He cursed. "It's too heavy!"

"Do it!"

"I can't by myself."

"Don't kill me!"

"Shut up!" Damien grabbed a fistful of the driver's shirt, hauled him up, smashed the barrel of the .38 across his head, and let his unconscious body slump back into the seat.

Damien tucked the gun into his pocket and ran around to Stone, who grabbed one handle, Damien the other. Each reached under the box to support it and began hauling it out. They grunted with effort, straining as they hustled back to the Chevy.

Armstrong hit a button on the dash and the trunk popped open. Traffic continued flowing past, nobody stopping. Armstrong had one hand on the horn, watching his rearview mirror for any police units.

"It's too heavy!" Ted Stone said. They were between

the courier's car and the Chevy, almost waddling with the weight of the strongbox between then, grunting and straining.

"Don't stop!" Damien shouted.

They grunted and strained some more and reached the back of the Ford, setting the strongbox on the lip of the trunk and inching it in. It dropped in with a thud, the rear of the Ford sinking a little. Damien ran back into the car as Stone slammed the trunk.

Armstrong was backing up before Damien had his door shut, then he wrenched the wheel over and sped back into traffic.

They had a half-hour before they had to see the fence. No way Damien was going to carry the strongbox into the place, so Armstrong parked in an alley and Damien opened the trunk, grabbed a hammer they'd brought along, and smashed the box's lock. He opened the lid and began taking out the individual boxes inside, loading them into a big laundry bag they'd put in the trunk earlier.

Armstrong drove the Ford to a furniture store called Denterman's. The front of the store was all wide-pane windows, showing off the showroom floor. Salespeople talked to customers, pointing out the features of various pieces of furniture.

Armstrong turned left, passing the front of the store, then made a quick right into the narrow alley behind it. They got out, each carrying a laundry sack. Damien pounded on a door marked Private, Keep Locked and they waited.

The door cracked open. A man stuck his head out and said, "Yeah?"

"I'm Damien. Gary's waiting for me."

The man pulled his head back in and shut the door. The gang waited, looking around, and the door opened again. The man stepped back and let them come in. He patted them all down, took their revolvers, and ushered them along a dark, narrow hallway that smelled of furniture polish.

The man turned left down another short hallway and knocked on a door. He opened it partway, said something to the guy inside, and pushed the door open. Damien, Stone, and Armstrong went in.

The large office had muted lighting, not much furniture, and bare walls. Gary Canno sat behind a bare table. He stood up and said hello as the three men put their bags on the top.

"Good work, gentlemen," Canno said. "Want a beer or anything?"

"I want a beer," Stone said.

Canno went to a small 'fridge in a corner, grabbed three beers, and handed them to the guys. They found some chairs and sat around the table while Canno began unloading each of the laundry bags.

Canno used a small bolt-cutter to cut open the mini-strongboxes, then spread out one of the laundry bags and began dumping the jewels out onto it, making a big pile. Damien, Stone, and Armstrong sat without talking, drinking beer and watching as Canno examined each stone with an eyepiece, nodding in satisfaction.

It took two hours to go through the stones, and after he finished, Canno took the eyepiece out and looked at the trio in front of him.

"One-point-two-million, my friends."

"That's a good haul," Armstrong stated.

"More than we thought," Stone said.

"When can we have the cash?" Damien said.

"It will take another hour. I don't have that much here. I'll have my guy go get it. You can either stay here and hang out, or there's a great burger joint across the street."

"We'll stay," Damien said.

"Hey, don't sweat it," Canno said. "If you want to eat, I'll go with you."

"Let's eat, then," Damien said.

"What happened to your neck?" Canno said.

"Don't ask."

The group left the office and moved across the street for lunch. There was more than food on Damien's mind. The jewel heist wasn't about filling his pockets, although it would. The money was more important than that.

The money would finance their next job.

Their biggest score yet.

CHAPTER TWENTY-SEVEN

Stiletto wasn't sure what to say to Chloe.

He wasn't sure he needed to say anything to Chloe. About her father, that is. Erin Keene had made it clear Chloe and her father weren't talking, a statement that resonated with Stiletto in ways the detective didn't understand.

He ate breakfast in the hotel dining room, ham and eggs with hash browns and toast and a small pot of green tea with a squeeze of lemon. The wall-mounted television had the morning news playing, the sound off but subtitles displayed, and Stiletto watched the footage of a highway incident that involved the theft of very expensive jewels and the assault of the courier in charge of them. Stiletto swallowed a bite of eggs. That was what the map in the lot above the Shipwreck Bar related to—the gang's robbery plans. What else were they planning? Scott hadn't seen indications of other jobs.

He finished breakfast and sat back with a sense of guilt. He should have eaten at Chloe's, but he wasn't sure he was ready to see her. Had Chloe always known more than she let on?

Finally, he decided the heck with it and left the hotel for his rental. It took twenty minutes to reach Chloe's Diner. He parked on the street in a spot vacated by a delivery truck.

The tables were full, as were most of the counter spots. An open stool at the end of the counter caught his eye and he migrated toward it, nodding at the waitresses who noticed him and raising an eyebrow at one, who said Chloe was in back and she'd be right out.

The cooks hustled behind the grill, the sharp smacks of spatulas on stainless steel mingling with the sizzles of frying breakfast meals that were carried out to tables as fast as the orders were placed. A waitress took Stiletto's order for a cup of tea and he asked for an apple pastry to go with it, even though he was full from his hotel breakfast.

He'd taken two bites when Chloe finally found him at the end of the counter. She wore her hair back, as usual, but rebellious strands dangled.

"That's all you're eating?"

He managed a grin. The weight he felt over the coming conversation didn't allow much more of a reaction.

Her face fell a little. She sensed a problem, he realized.

"Been busy?"

"I don't know where to start with how busy," he said. "But I probably shouldn't, you know."

"Not now, of course." She glanced down the counter at her patrons, who were too busy eating or talking or watching the TV news to pay attention to their conversation.

She turned to Scott. "Don't leave without saying goodbye."

"I won't."

Scott watched her walk away and felt lousy.

Had her father ordered Shelly Pierce's murder? Or, as he suspected, had the decision rested only with the wild bunch? Had Shelly learned of a planned crime like the freeway jewel heist and required removal? Her boyfriend, too? Stiletto shook his head as he stared at his pastry. That scenario really didn't make much sense. Her murder and Chad's murder had to be the result of something much bigger. Something that had already taken place. Too much time had gone by since her murder for the event not to have already happened.

When a booth opened, he moved into that, sitting against a wall and looking out the window at the passing traffic and street scenery. Presently business slowed down, and Stiletto asked a waitress if Chloe could come out and talk.

Chloe sat down across from him moments later.

"All right," she said, "out with it."

"You read minds?"

"I know when something's wrong. You wear it like a rug."

Stiletto said nothing.

"Well? What's it about?"

"It's about your father."

Any bluster Chloe had melted. She moved back a little from the table.

"What do you know?" she said.

"Tell me why he didn't want you involved in Justice for Jane."

"I'm not sure I wanted to know, really. Who told you about him?"

"Erin Keene."

Chloe closed her eyes and let out a sigh. She leaned forward again. "Only the cops know, I guess. It's not common knowledge anywhere else."

"She told me all about his syndicate connections."

"Connections? Is that what she told you? Scott, my father is the syndicate as far as Twin Falls is concerned."

"Did he have Shelly murdered?"

She blinked and her cheeks flushed, but she kept her resolve. "I don't think so. I think he's helping in the cover-up, though."

"Why?"

"I don't know. He and I aren't exactly on speaking

terms, and it's not something I can simply call up and ask him."

Stiletto drank some tea. He didn't have the appetite to finish the pastry. It remained on the small plate, with scattered crumbs.

"He showed up at my apartment the other night."

"Why?"

"He wanted to know who you were."

"Who told him about me? The cop?"

"Boskowictz, yeah. That's what I figured, anyway."

"What did you say?"

She stammered a little but said, "That you weren't a threat. And I know I shouldn't have said that. It just came out."

"It's okay. I haven't noticed anybody following me. It doesn't hurt that he might know about me."

"What are you going to do, Scott?"

The question hit Stiletto hard, right in the chest. If she didn't know what he was, she had a very clear idea. He probably resembled some of the men her father kept on hand. He didn't want to know for sure. But Chloe Giordana knew a killer when she saw one.

He didn't answer her.

"I don't like my father," she said, "but I don't want him dead, either."

"He's trying to locate Monica for you."

Her mouth dropped open. "What?"

"Maybe he's not as bad as you think."

"You think I should make amends?"

"All I know is that I wish my daughter would call me, and I have a feeling your father is the same way."

"What do you mean?"

"I mean, I have a kid, too. For some reason, she's not talking to me, and never returns my calls. I call on Christmas and her birthday. I can't even hear her voice on the voicemail greeting; it's just her number. I'd like to know what I've done to deserve this."

"I didn't know, Scott."

"Because I didn't tell you. It's okay."

"Is that why you've taken such an interest? Because Shelly reminds you—"

"No," he said. "I told you why. I was supposed to give her a message. Instead, I'm trying to solve her murder."

She didn't say anything.

Stiletto filled the silence. "All I want is the person who killed Shelly. So far, it doesn't look like your father's directly involved. As in, he didn't commit the murder or order it done, but maybe he knows the truth. Maybe he's waiting for somebody to ask him."

"Promise me," she said, "you won't go asking by sticking a gun in his face. He has plenty of men of his own."

"Men like me?"

"Exactly like you."

CHAPTER TWENTY-EIGHT

Chloe returned to her cramped office and shut the door.

She sat heavily in her chair and let out a curse at the pile on her desk. Re-order forms. Tax paperwork. The odds and ends that concerned all small business owners, and she wished she had somebody else to deal with all of it. The half-mug of coffee that had been sitting with the papers for two days testified that she wasn't on top of her tasks. Where had she been for the last two days?

She stopped. That wasn't where her focus needed to be at that moment. She was trying to avoid dealing with the thoughts in her head, but dodging them wasn't going to make her situation any easier. She had to get her mind sorted. With an elbow on the left chair arm, she covered her face with a hand and let out a sigh.

Stiletto's news had shocked her. For some reason, she had assumed her father had written her and Monica out of his life when Chloe took her leave. She should have known that even a pirate like Ben Giordana would retain a soft spot for his own flesh and blood.

She didn't hate her father, and she didn't want to see him dead, but she hated his lies. She hated that his ill-gotten gains had raised her and put her through school. Provided a lifestyle that had set her apart from her peers because at least they had known how their parents had earned their money.

He made her feel ashamed. Who had been harmed, or killed, in her father's pursuit of a dollar? There was so much she didn't know, so much she was afraid to think about. It was the reason she had been so insistent on forging her own way with the diner. She didn't want any blood money associated with her name.

And now her father was looking for his granddaughter, using his dirty resources where Chloe was powerless to do so. Conflicting emotions ran through her. She wanted Monica home. She had no way of getting her home. All she could do was wait for drunken phones calls or a sober moment when she finally boarded a bus for Twin Falls and came back to sort out her life. But her father had men who might find her. She might be reunited with her father via the blood money she so much wanted to avoid.

Stiletto had had no idea what he was talking about when he'd said her father might not be that bad. There was no doubt in Chloe's mind that he was "that bad." Stiletto was speaking as a father who missed his daughter, who seemed not to have the same option as she. Monica would more than likely come home, but Stiletto didn't appear to have that option. That was when the two distinct situations melded into one. That was when she started to sob.

Stiletto returned to the Hyatt with a take-away bag of food from the diner. He knocked on her hotel room door using the agreed-upon pattern that identified him as not being a threat. Erin opened the door and smiled.

"How are you feeling?" he said as she let him inside. She pushed the door shut and took the bag from his hand before he offered it to her.

"A little better," she said, crossing to the table to open the bag. Stiletto had bought her a BLT and French fries. She started eating.

Stiletto shifted uncomfortably. The open drapes on the window shouldn't have bothered him, but they did, and he had to consider Erin's point of view. She wanted them open to let in the light and the window cracked to let in the outside air. He cleared his throat and joined her at the table.

"This is good," Erin said between bites.

"Been back to your house?"

"Long enough to get the window repair guy and cleaners going."

"How long are you going to stay here?"

"Not much longer. I think I'll go home in a day or two. Work told me to stay away for a few days."

"Are they looking into what happened?"

"I haven't asked."

"Do you think they are?"

"I'm sure. They'll do enough to identify the shooters. When they ask questions, somebody will tell them to stand down."

Stiletto scooted back from the table to be out of view of the windows.

"What is it with you and windows?" she said.

"Paranoia never killed anybody twice."

"You realize," she said, licking stray salt from a French fry off a finger, "that you're more vulnerable on the street than in your hotel room?"

"Maybe, but I'm more alert on the street than in the hotel room. We should be able to relax in our sanctuaries."

"Until they ambush you there," she said.

"You have a point."

She swallowed another bite of her sandwich. "But that's not what you came here to talk about."

"No," he said. "I came to check on you and go over a few things. Did you hear about that freeway jewel robbery?"

"Of course."

"Our little wild bunch is responsible."

Stiletto explained his entry into the loft above the Shipwreck Bar, where he found the map detailing the travel route and location of the smash-and-grab.

"Are you aware of how many laws your broke doing that?" she asked.

"Are you aware the law has about as much power in this town as a snail pushing a boulder?"

"Touché." She ate a French fry.

"I can confirm Joe Armstrong as one of the gang members, and the fellow Damien, but there are two others. They were short one last night, which means I may have put one of them in the hospital, or they're keeping him somewhere else while he recovers from the beating I dished out."

She didn't reply.

"Is there a way you can check?"

She put her sandwich down. "I'm supposed to be taking a few days off."

"Erin, we can't fool around. I don't know if you're afraid to talk to your friends at work or if you think there's truly nothing you can do, but you're my only resource here. We aren't going to find out what happened by staying in our seats."

He stopped talking and waited for her answer.

CHAPTER TWENTY-NINE

"I can make a few calls," she said, "but I can't make any promises. You're going to have to do most of the legwork yourself."

Stiletto nodded. Maybe that was the best way. Maybe asking somebody who had been smacked down for so long was asking too much. Erin Keene wasn't the typical example of somebody living with the boot of oppression on their neck, but it showed in her actions. She might have been correct in that they couldn't use police resources for Stiletto's private vendetta, but pissed-off cops could get a lot done despite restrictions. Erin Keene focused only on the restrictions because she was afraid to awaken the giant who might fully step on her neck.

Erin Keene had shown the spark of defiance once when she'd released him from jail. She had known what she was doing then, but the result had placed a target on her back. Instead of increasing her resolve, the murder attempt was making her shrink. She was thinking about it too much, letting it wear her down inside.

Stiletto didn't blame her, but he needed her help. He had to guide her through the next step of resistance, the one that would get her out from under the oppressor's boot and give her enough time to stick a knife in the neck of the ones using Twin Falls, Idaho as their own kingdom and treating the citizens like peasants.

He knew where to find Joe Armstrong. Where there was one, there would surely be the others. It was only a question of how much time he'd require to accomplish the goal.

"I appreciate anything you can do, of course," Stiletto said. "I know you're taking a risk."

"A bigger risk than I realized I was taking when I got you out of jail."

Stiletto nodded. She'd confirmed his diagnosis, but instead of a sense of accomplishment, he felt bad. Especially for her. She didn't need him to tell her the score. She knew it already, and the knowledge probably ate away at her guts.

It was a condition with which nobody could live.

"You became a cop for noble reasons, Erin," he said. "This is Tina's case all over again. We have to stop what's going on in this city."

Her eyes moistened. She nodded.

"I'll try," she said.

For now, that was enough.

"I want to get pictures of the gang," he told her. "At least the ones still on the street."

"Do you think Shelly or her boyfriend was killed over a crime as simple as a jewel robbery, or something similar?"

"No, I think it was much bigger than that. Whatever it was has probably already taken place. We have to find out what it was and act accordingly."

"Bodies in the street?"

"Oh, I'm leaving bodies behind me, don't you worry."

"And me to clean them up?"

"When you're done, Twin Falls will be great again."

"What's at the top of the food chain? Who is behind the cover-up? You might be facing more than you realize."

Stiletto laughed. "I've faced worse, believe me."

"I think you think you have. Twin Falls is where the enemy is part of the DNA. You can't simply use a scalpel to slice it out."

"Once I can prove Damien and his gang killed Shelly, everything else will line up in my sights."

"You sure?"

"Every enemy I've ever faced," Stiletto said, "has one thing in common."

"What's that?"

"Knock out the foundation, and their kingdom comes tumbling down."

She had no answer for that. Stiletto sat quietly while she finished her sandwich.

Vince "Six" Coburn turned off the Mercedes and looked across the street.

The Tom Tom Club occupied prime real estate at Addison Avenue and Grandview Drive. Brightly lit in front, the lights acted as a beacon in an otherwise-vacant area, with mostly open country and farmland beyond. There were some spots of light in the dark backdrop, but the Tom Tom Club overpowered those flickers.

Six watched from the parking lot across the street as patrons flocked to the open doors of the club. Doormen in red uniforms stood on either side of the doors, welcoming the guests. The marquee above the door advertised the night's entertainment, a country band that made a circuit of the Midwest and returned to Twin Falls two or three times a year. Six didn't particularly care for country music, although he held the view that one could tell who was truly an American by whether or not they appreciated the music of Johnny Cash. Forget ICE and border enforcement. Whoever didn't groove to The Best of Cash wasn't worthy of living in the United States.

He'd let the regular folks determine if the traveling band was worthwhile. He'd come for something else entirely, a task none of the guests would want to know about.

Six reached under his coat and withdrew a SIG-Sauer P-225A1 semi-auto pistol. The compact automatic with its eight rounds of 9mm firepower warmed in his hand as he checked the load and confirmed a round in the firing chamber. The extra-length barrel had threading on the extended portion to take a sound suppressor. Six pulled the black tube from another pocket and screwed it on. It fit back in his holster properly, but the suppressor poked into his side. Hazards of the job.

Six left the Mercedes and crossed the street. It was a warm night. He was wearing his steel-toed shoes again, and they were comfortable indeed. He felt sweat on the back of his neck. The big man wore a gray suit this time, his polished shoes tapping on the pavement. The right-side doorman wished him a good evening, and Six returned the greeting.

He entered the Tom Tom Club with the eyes of a shark, mentally sorting the bad guys from the regular people.

Tim Dell might be the man in the office, the one everybody knew as the owner who made the day-to-day decisions, but Six knew the truth. Kurt Swanberg might have only owned a percentage of the club, but he behaved like he owned all of it and Dell was his yes-man. Six had no illusions about any other arrangement, hence his need for the gun. He was stepping into enemy territory. He had to be prepared for the worst.

CHAPTER THIRTY

Six no longer drank alcohol. He was eighteen years sober, and being around booze wasn't easy. Giordana had asked him many times why he didn't seem to be listening during meetings. He was listening, but he was also repeating "one day at a time" in his head so as not to touch any liquor.

When he reached the bar, he asked the bartender for a Coke. The bartender didn't blink an eye. Six received his drink and told the bartender to keep the change from his ten-dollar bill. Six leaned against the bar to take in the scenery. He wasn't sure what kind of security arrangements the club had. The bouncer was obvious, positioned near the door, but that was only one man. Six wanted to know who else was hanging around, armed or not, to deal with trouble.

The Tom Tom Club was divided into three parts, which were tiered. The large bar area followed the length of a wall and sat on a raised platform overlooking the dining area. There were tables for maybe a hundred couples. Reservations were a must at the club. A step down from the dining area was the dance floor and bandstand. The dance floor was currently empty, but the stage was crowded with technicians setting up audio equipment and musicians testing the equipment, although their impromptu jamming session to test the functionality of their gear was muted and not blasting into the rest of the club. The band had another hour before they began their show, and the pre-show on the stage wasn't attracting much attention from the diners. Nobody at the bar glanced that way either.

As Six continued his scan, his eyes drifted upward to the ceiling, where hanging speakers promised to bathe the club in sound, while intersecting pipes testified to the building's air conditioning prowess.

What really caught Six's eye were the small cameras hidden among the intersecting pipes. The pipes might have cut off the view of some of the cameras' eyes, but those in other locations made up for the loss. Six stopped counting at ten. The whole club was under massive surveillance.

And Tim Dell and his staff weren't simply watching for troublemakers. They were looking for guys like him who weren't supposed to be there, whose presence suggested problems on a larger scale than a drunken guest who reacted poorly to a woman's refusal to dance.

Six had finished most of his drink when two big bruisers approached him from either side. They wore sports jackets over business casual attire. The jackets remained unbuttoned because they needed access to the high-caliber hardware underneath. Six knew the look. He used it himself.

"Get out," said the bruiser on the left.

"Drop dead," Six said. "I'm a paying customer."

"The boss wants you to leave, Six," Right Bruiser said.

Six turned to Right Bruiser. "I like you better. Tell me more."

"Dell doesn't know why you're here, and he doesn't want to know. You need to go."

"Or else what?"

"Or else we'll take you out the back way. That won't be pretty."

Six laughed. He downed the rest of his drink. Ice cubes clinked together. He set the glass on the bar and waved off the bartender's silent offer of a refill.

"I'm not here to jam up anybody," Six said. "I don't want trouble, either."

"Then come with us."

"I need to speak to Tim Dell. Tell him I'm on a peace mission. I only want to talk about a couple of things, and then I'll go out the same way I came in."

Right Bruiser said, "That's not the way it works."

"That's the way it's going to work," Six said, "otherwise you'll get trouble like you won't believe."

"You and what army?" Left Bruiser said.

Six looked left. "I'm glad you asked. Look around."

The two bruisers turned their heads left and right, then back to Six. "So?" said Right Bruiser.

"How many people do I have embedded in the dining area?"

"You came in alone," said Left Bruiser.

Six ignored the man. He kept his eyes on Righty. Righty said, "All right, Six. Hang here a minute. Get a refill if you want. I'll go talk to Dell."

"Going to leave your friend with me?" Six said.

"Yeah," said Righty. "You need a babysitter."

"I promise not to make a mess in my diaper," Six said to Righty's back, laughing as he caught a few odd glances from nearby bar patrons.

Six looked at Lefty.

"Can you count to ten?"

"Sure," said Lefty. "That's how many bullets I got in my gun. Want to see them? You'll need to dig them out of your ass, though."

Six laughed and shook his head. "I'll pass."

Presently Righty returned, but not with Tim Dell.

Righty returned with Sergeant Carl Boskowictz.

CHAPTER THIRTY-ONE

"I heard you were back," Boskowictz said. "Now get lost."

"Nice suit, Carl," Six said. "I'm not used to seeing you out of your uniform. Might want to lay off the meatloaf, though. You're coming out in the middle."

Boskowictz's pock-marked face twisted in anger. Six wanted him to throw a punch, but the police sergeant calmed down as fast as he'd become worked up.

"How many times do we have to tell you that you aren't wanted here, Vince? The band is almost ready to play. We don't want to mess up the customer experience."

"Listen to yourself, Carl," Six said. "You're nothing like you used to be."

Boskowictz stepped closer to Six, almost nose to nose with him. Six felt the heat radiating from the big man.

"I'm better than I used to be."

Six didn't flinch. "Nuts. You're an errand boy talking

about customer experience. This is what happens when you bite the hand that feeds you, Carl. The grass ain't greener after all, is it?"

"It can't be much better where you are. How hard is it to bump off a cop and a stranger?"

"That stranger ain't no stranger," Six said. "That's what I'm trying to find out."

"By asking Dell?"

"By asking questions of everybody, yeah. Tell Tim I only want to talk."

"Tim ain't talking to anybody tonight. Except me, to tell you to get your Scotch ass out of our club."

Six sighed. Boskowictz backed off.

"All right, Carl. If that's the way it has to be."

"That's the way it is."

"What does Swanberg have on Ben?"

Boskowictz blinked in surprise. "What?"

"What's Swanberg blackmailing Ben with?"

"None of your business."

"As soon as I find out the score, you're going to wish you'd never changed sides."

"Good luck."

Vince Six straightened his coat. He nodded good-bye to Lefty and Righty, ignoring Boskowictz, and exited via the front door. There was a line of people waiting to get in now, and the doormen were busier than when Six had arrived.

Typical night at the Tom Tom Club.

Tim Dell's hands shook as he left the club via the back door and crossed the employee parking lot to his Maserati Ghibli four-door at the very end. The night was over. The cleaning crew was still inside, the front doors open for air circulation, and all the other employees were long gone. As Dell crossed the blacktop, the world was only him, some crickets, and the nighttime chill.

The visit from Vince Six bothered him. What the heck did Giordana want to talk to him about? Dell would have to report the visit to Swanberg. He knew Boskowictz would say something, which meant if Dell didn't, Kurt would want to know what he was hiding, so first thing in the morning Dell had to call the boss on the hill and report the visit and the result. He hoped the animosity between Giordana and Swanberg wasn't heating up again. Six had said he was on a peace mission, but that didn't make sense either. If Giordana wanted a meeting, he could call Swanberg directly. They weren't strangers to each other. There was no need for go-betweens or beating around the bush.

The Maserati Ghibli was a nice car, one that Dell had coveted for a long time, but the car company had fallen behind as far as luxury and performance car tech was concerned. Dell still needed a key fob to unlock the doors, and a key unfolded from the fob that had to be inserted into the ignition, same as a Toyota truck only the poor people could afford. But the car said Maserati on the back, and for Dell, that was enough.

He removed the fob from his pocket and pressed the button that snapped out the key.

He pressed the button to unlock the driver's door. The car's front and rear lamps flashed as the locks clicked. Dell tossed his briefcase in the back seat and opened the driver's door.

"Hold it, Tim."

Tim Dell cursed. The voice had come from his right. Dell slowly turned. Standing near a lamppost on the sidewalk was Vince Six. Six left the lamppost and stepped onto the blacktop.

"Get in the car."

"Vince—"

Dell gasped as Six's right hand flashed in and out of his coat and jammed the cold muzzle of a SIG-Sauer automatic into his belly.

"I tried being nice," Six said. "Now get in the car. You don't have your goons to look out for you anymore."

Dell winced as Six pried the key fob from Dell's hand. The man's grip was solid, and he rubbed his right hand afterward.

"Dammit, Vince." Dell scowled as he slid behind the wheel of the four-door.

Vince Six put away his gun and joined him on the passenger side.

"Shut your door."

Dell obeyed. The interior of the car was quiet and comfortable, and Dell wondered what was going to happen next.

"I told your guys I only wanted to talk," Six said, "and you've made me wait all night for you. Now I'm not happy."

Dell didn't look at Six. His eyes faced forward.

"Too bad."

"Well, too bad for somebody," Six agreed.

"You're here. Tell me what you want."

"I'm here about Swanberg. And what he has on Ben Giordana."

"I don't know what you're talking about."

Dell screamed as two fingers pinched his right earlobe. He twisted in the seat, slapping at Six's grip.

"Feel like talking?"

"Okay! Okay!"

Six let go, and Dell rubbed his earlobe. He finally made eye contact.

"What's the deal, Six? You know Ben doesn't have a leg to stand on."

"That's what I'm here for. What does Swanberg have on Ben? Why the conflict?"

"What do you want to know for?"

"I'm trying to solve some problems. I can't solve those problems without knowing why Ben is shutting me out on matters related to Swanberg."

"And what makes you think I'm going to tell you? I work for Swanberg, dummy! Boskowictz has probably already told him you came by tonight. Now I have to tell him you not only came by the club but then braced me in the car. Do you know what position I'm in?"

"Sounds like a rock and a hard place."

"Sure. And if I don't have a good explanation—"

Six held up a hand. "That's the thing, Tim. For somebody who only owns a small interest in your club, he sure exerts a lot of control over you."

"I like breathing."

"How'd you like to be out from under Swanberg for good and working for Ben?"

"Fat chance of that."

"I'm serious. You help us, we'll help you."

"Swanberg would have to be dead."

"I never said that wasn't the goal, Tim."

"You're serious?"

"Yeah. Ben's in a bad way. We need to get this sorted. You can be rewarded for helping or go crying to your daddy while telling yourself it's your choice to do so."

"This is too much, man, I don't know."

"Think it over."

"I'll need a couple of days."

Vince Six checked his watch. "You have two minutes."

CHAPTER THIRTY-TWO

"I need reassurances," Tim Dell said.

"Tim, you have my assurance that I won't kill you tonight."

"Not that, idiot! Can I keep the club? Do I get another if Swanberg lasts long enough to burn it down?"

"You're making my point, Tim."

"I know, I know! Swanberg is human garbage, I get it. I told you I like breathing, and I'll be doing a lot less of it if Swanberg even gets a whiff about me talking to you."

"Better hope Boskowictz isn't watching us."

Dell jerked around in his seat, craning his neck out the window. "Is he?"

Vince Six quietly chuckled.

Dell glared at him.

"Any more of that crap and you can kick rocks."

Six's smile faded. "No more, I promise. Now give me details."

Tim Dell let out a deep breath and turned his attention back to the steering wheel, his head tilted toward the center emblem.

"What happened goes back a gazillion years," Dell said, "to when Giordana and Swanberg got out of high school here in Twin Falls. Swanberg was pursuing his computer stuff, but he was running a numbers racket on the side. Giordana was already part of the outfit. He'd been in the Tornado gang for a bunch of years and got recruited that way."

"Uh-huh."

"Well, one night, Swanberg witnessed a murder. Giordana had to prove his worth, right? The outfit told him to go and pull an off job on a guy that was cheating them out of a few grand a month, okay? Problem is, the guy was a customer of Swanberg's, and when Swanberg went to collect money the guy owned from playing the numbers, he saw Giordana stick a knife in the guy's neck."

"That's it?"

"That's it, man. Straight gospel. You can look it up. The killing went unsolved, and all these years later, when Giordana is top dog and Swanberg is back in town with his millions, he told Giordana he'd seen the whole thing, and Giordana had better look the other way on some things, or Swanberg would rat to the feds. Your buddy has been kowtowing to Swanberg ever since, while Swanberg's kid runs around raising ten kinds of hell."

"I know about the kid."

"Ever wonder what the robberies are all about?"

"I've wondered."

"Think drugs, man. I'm talking a flood of the stuff leaving Twin Falls for the Midwest, and Giordana gets none of the cut. If he's really unlucky, he'll have to explain to New York what the situation is, and that'll cost him. It's in Ben's best interests to look the other way, brush things under the rug, and try to stay alive long enough to get out of the rackets."

"And you know all this how?"

"Swanberg likes to gloat. It's how he got Boskowictz to work for him, too. He keeps an eye on Ben to make sure he doesn't do anything stupid, like try to kill Swanberg. Ben can't do anything about it."

"Uh-huh."

"And I'll tell you another thing Ben doesn't know," Dell said.

"Okay."

"If anything happens to him, the evidence comes out. It's in a wall safe behind his desk in that big mansion of his."

"You mean it was in a wall safe behind his desk in that big mansion of his."

Dell's face turned white.

"What are you talking about, Six?"

"I mean, you're going to tell me the layout of the place, everything you know, and you're going to drop a dime the next time Swanberg leaves the place. Get it?"

Dell gulped.

"I didn't say it was going to be easy, Dell." Six smiled. "Have a good night."

Six exited the Maserati and gently pushed the passenger door closed. Dell at least appreciated that. Too many slammed the door, and that hurt the car. He was always telling people to be easy on his doors. But nobody—

Stop!

Dell's hands were really shaking now.

He started the car and drove out of the parking lot.

He sure hoped Boskowictz wasn't hiding in the parking lot. He wouldn't survive the night if the sergeant witnessed anything.

Vince Six kept the SIG-Sauer in his right hand as he crossed the empty street to the customer parking lot. He didn't think he'd be ambushed at this point, but if he wasn't ready for such a thing, he'd fall victim to one for sure.

His eyes darted left and right all the way to his car. When he was behind the wheel, he jammed the gun under his left leg. He didn't relax until the engine was running and he was on the road.

He processed the conversation. Of course, it would be something simple. Six never would have guessed the blackmail was as simple as Dell described.

Now he had to figure out how to use the information, and how to get at the stuff in the safe. What could Swanberg have? It had to be solid evidence; otherwise, it was one man's word against another regarding the ancient murder.

Six planned to find out.

CHAPTER THIRTY-THREE

Stiletto started early the next morning. He didn't know where Joe Armstrong lived and assumed he would be at his parents' home. Stiletto staked out the Shipwreck Bar because undoubtedly Armstrong, Damien, or the other crony would show up. What Scott really wanted to do was brace the fellow still in the hospital, and hopefully, Erin would come through with a name and room number.

But Stiletto had no confidence in the police force of Twin Falls. Erin could make all the calls she felt comfortable with, but there was a high chance of her running into the same roadblock she'd put up in front of him—fear of going forward because of the consequences. The department was well aware of what had happened at Erin's home. If anybody she spoke with had a family, zipped lips wouldn't open, no matter what manner of persuasion was employed.

The goon in the hospital was vulnerable and might answer questions about Shelly. Failing that, Stiletto could grab one of the other three. He wanted to know who Damien was. All he had was a first name, nothing else. The only way he knew how to do that was via surveillance. That had its own risks, but Stiletto had a way of handling any issues.

The Colt Combat Government .45 auto was nestled under his left arm, covered by his jacket.

The time for keeping the artillery hidden had passed. The enemy was ready for war, so Stiletto had to be equally prepared.

Stiletto waited down the street from the bar. It didn't open until eleven in the morning, so he had a few hours before the early customers showed up, but the rest of the neighborhood around him was alive. The auto repair shop was busy, and the other businesses that were a stone's throw from where Stiletto sat on the side of the road were open and active. Scott waited behind the wheel, smoking a cigar. Since he wasn't a litterbug, he tapped the ash into a Coke can he'd cut in half. The partial can was in the rental's cup holder. If the rental company wanted to yell at him later for ignoring the no-smoking sign, that was their business. Scott could more than afford the advertised $250 cleaning fee.

A Challenger pulled into the side lot of the Shipwreck, and a lone figure jumped out and climbed the steps to the upper loft. Stiletto would have tried to intercept the man, but the Challenger's engine rumbled, the driver's door partway open. Scott started the rental. By the time the figure hustled down the steps, Scott had the car in gear. The man's face was clear to Scott as he climbed into the Challenger.

Damien.

Stiletto let the Challenger go up the street and turn left, then followed quickly behind. He had to wait for a few cars to go by before making the right turn, but the congestion on the roadway made it easy to catch up with the Challenger, and also covered Stiletto's presence. As they drove, Scott noted Damien's refusal to follow even basic evasion maneuvers. He didn't think anybody was behind him or would want to be.

Stiletto followed the Challenger up Eastland Drive to a hook where a left turn brought them onto East 4100. After another short distance, the Challenger pulled into the south parking entrance of the sprawling Magic Valley Mall.

It wasn't hard to find a parking spot. There weren't a lot of cars taking up space on the blacktop. Stiletto parked a few rows down from the Challenger and watched Damien in the rearview mirror as he left the muscle car and proceeded toward the mall building. After a minute, Scott followed.

The south lot faced the rear of the mall building, with unmarked doorways leading inside and loading docks on either end. The docks were filled with semi-trucks unloading product shipments.

Damien was a man on a mission as he pushed through

a set of double doors. Scott hung back for a minute, then followed. They had entered via an exit and were in what seemed to be the armpit of the mall, where boutique shops had to fight for visibility via signs in the main walkway ahead. Maybe their rent was better in that spot.

Damien didn't stop to look in any shop windows as Stiletto trailed behind him. Canned Muzak filled the interior, thankfully at a low volume. There were also a large number of people, obviously of retirement age, who were power-walking on the upper and lower floors. Morning was the best time for that. They could get their exercise and catch up, and afterward, get a sweet roll and a coffee. Judging by the size of some of them, they needed to do more than power-walk to stay in shape.

But there weren't enough people for Stiletto to get close. He had to stay back and duck into alcoves and watch Damien from a distance. He wasn't hard to track or difficult to catch up with. When he turned into the upper-level food court, Stiletto was glad. Now he'd be in one spot for a while. Or maybe a long while, since he sat down with Joe Armstrong and a third man at a table. There was a pile of sweet rolls and several cups of coffee on the table. Damien pulled something from his pocket. A smartphone, Stiletto noticed as he ordered a cup of green tea from one of the vendors, found a stray newspaper sports section, and took a table far enough away, where he hoped they wouldn't notice him.

Using the newspaper for concealment, he snapped pictures of the trio with his own smartphone. He wasn't sure what value the pictures would have. Maybe Erin could supply some information once she saw their faces. He could for sure run them by Shelly's diner co-workers and friends, Penny and Vicki.

Stiletto sipped his tea, pretended to care about what he was reading (since the efforts of a bunch of millionaire athletes really didn't impress him), and waited to see what he might learn from the wild bunch at the other table.

CHAPTER THIRTY-FOUR

Damien Swanberg dropped into the plastic chair.

"What's up?" he said. He didn't look at Joe Armstrong or Teddy Stone as they sat across from him. He took out his phone, clicked on the gallery app, and filled the smartphone's screen with a picture.

"How's Eric doing?" Teddy Stone asked. "Anybody check on him?"

"I haven't," Damien said. He set his phone down.

"His sister told me he should be out in a day or two," Joe Armstrong said.

"Uh-huh," Damien said. He broke off a piece of sweet roll and ate it.

"So what's the decision on Ivy and his kid?" Teddy Stone said.

"They won't negotiate," Damien said. "My father wants them out of here. If we're going to be in a position to take over once Giordana goes tits up, we have to pull this off."

"Let's see the pics," Armstrong said.

Damien picked up his phone again and turned the screen toward his friends. Damien started scrolling through pictures.

"The team we hired with the jewel money has been tracking Peter Ivy since we hired them," Damien said, "and they have his movements mapped. Dude has a routine and sticks with it. We can move in any time."

Damien had seen the pictures often enough to know them by heart. Peter Ivy leaving the house, going to school, work, and various other daily stops. The pictures showed him meeting his father Roger at Club Ivy for work.

The team of shooters Damien had hired, who had no previous connection to Twin Falls or his father, had conducted their surveillance well.

"Is the cabin ready?" Armstrong said.

The plan was to kidnap Peter Ivy and make his father turn over a drug operation to the Swanberg wild bunch, and ultimately to Damien's father to run alongside any drug interests Ben Giordana had. They wanted to eventually force Giordana out of the drug business and out of Twin Falls.

Damien's crew had secured a cabin north of town, near Snake River, to stash Peter Ivy while they communicated demands to his father.

"We're all set," Damien said. "The question is whether we wait for Eric. What do you think?" He put away his phone.

"It would be wrong to not have Eric involved," Teddy Stone said. "He came up with the plan."

"Okay," Damien said. "We'll hang back for a few days."

"What about our mystery man?" Joe Armstrong asked.

Damien let out a breath. "Somebody let him out of jail."

"Who?"

"A detective. I've been told not to interfere with her. My father has plans of his own."

"What does that mean?" Armstrong said.

"It means he didn't tell me anything, like always." Damien said. "I can't tell you what I don't know, except that it's our asses if we get involved. Let my old man handle it."

"You know something, Damien," Armstrong said. "It's all over your face. Your poker façade sucks."

Damien tapped on the table. He broke off another piece of sweet roll but set it down.

"Spill," said Stone.

"I only know this from Boskowictz," Damien said, leaning closer to his friends. "Our mystery man and Giordana's daughter are pretty tight. He's here looking for whoever killed Shelly Pierce."

Teddy Stone let out a curse.

"That explains a lot," Joe Armstrong said.

"Yeah." Damien leaned back in his chair again. "Now we know why he's here. Where we might find him is the next question."

"We need to get rid of the guy before we grab Ivy," Armstrong said. "He's probably already been to Club Ivy to see what they know. Hell, they might have told him about us."

"We wouldn't be walking around if Ivy had, Joe. Relax," Damien said. "I think Ivy said enough to cover his ass but turn Mystery Man in our direction."

"I'll break his kid's ribs for that," Teddy Stone said.

The three stopped talking for a moment, a moment that stretched into two minutes before Damien said, "We gonna finish this stuff or toss it?"

"Toss it," Armstrong said. "I'm suddenly not very hungry."

"Yeah," Stone said. "Your old man better move fast, or our mystery friend is going to be a huge problem."

Damien glared at Stone, who remained stoic under the hard gaze.

"What are you going to do about it?" Stone said.

"Watch your mouth."

Stone scoffed.

"Cool it, guys. We got work to do," Armstrong said.

The three men rose from the table warily, Armstrong

acting as the go-between for Damien and Stone as they arranged the next meeting at the loft. The three men left in different directions.

Stiletto didn't leave his table.

The last bit of conversation seemed to antagonize the one called Damien, he noted. He wondered what the deal was. He sat and scrolled through the pictures he'd taken. All from the same angle, they weren't that great, but they did show enough of their faces that he could probably get a comment from Erin, if she knew of them, and if they'd had previous police contact.

He knew one thing for sure. They were planning another job, more people would be hurt, and the cops would look the other way. He had to find a way to stop the cycle and fast.

CHAPTER THIRTY-FIVE

Scott Stiletto didn't find Erin Keene at her hotel, so he drove by her home. He found her sitting on the step of the front porch, her knees up to her chest and her arms wrapped around her knees. She stared into the distance, which in this case wasn't much more than the other houses across the street, but the faraway gaze was familiar to Scott.

She snapped out of the daze as he approached.

"Are you okay?"

"Yeah," she said. She scooted over to give him room on the step. "All cleaned up and fixed, but it's strange being in there. But I'm going to force myself to stay here tonight."

"It might sound like a cliché, but I know how you feel."

"Really?"

"I came home from work once," Stiletto said, "and there was an assassin waiting for me. She tried to kill me with an automatic weapon and shot up my car instead."

"Wait, a what?"

Stiletto grinned. "That was another life."

She laughed. "One of these days, I need to hear the story of your life, Scott. I have a feeling it would make a great movie."

"Maybe, but the price of the rights would be pretty high."

She stopped laughing and let out a satisfied sigh. "I'm feeling much better," she said, "despite feeling weird inside the house."

"You'll be fine. Give it time."

"What did you do with your house?"

"I had to sell it when the CIA fired me."

"Another twist? Boy, you must have some story."

Stiletto took out his smartphone. He didn't want to dwell on his past, and his remarks, more joking than serious, were taking them down a road he wasn't willing to travel. Plus, there were things about his CIA life he couldn't talk about, that fell under the lifetime code of silence CIA officers swore to uphold. He'd done a lot of good in that job, although sometimes he'd done a lot of bad in the name of good.

"What's on your phone?" Erin Keene said.

"I followed our friends to the mall today. It looks like they're planning something."

He handed her the phone, and she scrolled through the pictures of the food court meeting that showed the trio at a single angle.

"It's a picture of three guys having breakfast," she said. "What do you expect me to say about this?"

Stiletto pointed to Damien and Armstrong and identified them. He said, "You told me Kurt Swanberg had a son named Damien. The same?"

"That's him."

"Good. I don't know who the third player is yet."

"So what?"

Stiletto bit off his frustration. From a legal perspective, he knew she was right, and he appreciated her pushback in some way, too. He couldn't simply start blasting without knowing he had the right people in front of his gun. This wasn't a war zone, it was Twin Falls, Idaho. He needed concrete evidence and facts about the guilt of the wild bunch before he acted. He also needed to know why they'd killed Shelly Pierce and her boyfriend.

And if they truly had.

He knew one thing for sure, though. He said, "These are the guys Shelly's friends told me about. The ones she was afraid of. The ones her boyfriend Chad was involved with. They specifically pointed out this Damien fellow as the one Shelly truly didn't like."

"Did you go see them?"

"Because I talked with Penny and Vicki before coming here, yes."

"All right. What you have is a bunch of guys that creeped out a couple of girls. That's more like any day at high school. In this case, maybe we have some guys in their twenties who are still in that socially awkward stage and don't know how to behave around women. What you don't have is any reason for an arrest warrant or whatever else you have in mind. I'm assuming you aren't simply going to shoot them and figure you're correct. You want proof, right?"

Stiletto didn't answer. He put away his phone and tried a different approach.

"Have you had any luck with the one still in the hospital?"

"Dodging my question?"

"No," he said. "I'm saving you from being an accessory."

She said, "Oh," in a startled way, then looked away for a minute. A moment of silence passed. Stiletto waited for her to answer his question.

"Well, I did have some luck seeing him at the hospital," she said. "I went there, badge and all, looking for an interview to see if he'd be interested in pressing charges."

"What did he tell you?"

"You whacked him really good. Were you fighting or tenderizing meat?"

"Maybe a bit of both."

"He's getting out in two days." she said.

"Really? Who's picking him up?"

"Wasn't any of my business. The point is, he's not interested in pressing charges. He says he didn't get a good look at you and couldn't identify you in the lineup if his life depended on it."

"Interesting."

"I thought so too. What do you think it means?"

"I think it means they can't afford any extra interference right now."

"Today's meeting at the mall was for the next job?"

"Yeah. I'm going to have to find out what kind of job, though. I know they pulled that jewel robbery, and I have a feeling the money is being used to finance this next deal."

"What gives you that idea?"

"That fact that they're planning another, considering how much those jewels were worth."

The wind blew. Erin Keene said she should add chimes to the porch. It might be nice to hear chimes when the wind blew.

"What about Doug Armstrong?" Stiletto said. "Did you dig there at all?"

"You're like a cat," she said. "One-track mind. Do you stare at doors until they open?"

"Does that work?"

She scoffed. "Doug Armstrong has no record or dirty dealings that we can discern, but he does know people in the city administration."

"Uh-huh."

"Which means he's probably dirty, but we can't connect him to Giordana."

"Okay."

"Don't be mad at me."

"I'm not mad, Erin."

"Disappointed?"

"No. I understand your situation. Nobody else wants to get hurt. I get it."

She looked away in shame.

"By the time I'm done here," Stiletto said, "you won't have to hide anymore."

She didn't look at him. "That almost makes me want to be an accessory to whatever you have planned."

"You won't like me when I'm done."

She turned to him. "I'm not sure I like you now."

Scott frowned.

Erin laughed.

CHAPTER THIRTY-SIX

Vince Six sat across from Ben Giordana on the balcony of the penthouse and didn't beat around the bush.

"What's up with the murder evidence Swanberg has on you?"

Giordana raised an eyebrow. "You've been busy."

"This situation has you in knots, Ben. Something's gotta give. We need to stop this."

Giordana sighed. He'd returned from a meeting with his lieutenants only a few minutes earlier, where Six had acted as bodyguard, and they sat on the balcony in his suit minus the jacket. The tie was gone, and the top button on his shirt was undone.

Giordana had seemed like his old self during the meeting, wearing his snappy suit, listening to the updates on operations and expected amounts of money coming from those operations. But now, back at home base, the veneer of the tough leader had gone, replaced by the thousand-yard stare Giordana had been wearing since Six returned.

Six did not like seeing his boss in this condition.

"It happened a long time ago, Vince."

"Did Swanberg witness the killing?"

"He has a picture."

"Really? That's news to me."

"Your source doesn't know everything. I think it was a setup. I was supposed to be doing an initiation into the outfit, but Swanberg was there to snap a picture. He knew to be there ahead of time, somehow. I never learned how. And whoever told him is long dead now."

Six said nothing.

"How did you find out about this?"

Six explained his visits with Osslo and especially Tim Dell at the Tom Tom Club.

"Dell knows where the evidence is hidden."

"Hell he does."

"Says Swanberg keeps it in a safe in his private office."

"No way, Vince."

"It's worth a try. Me and a couple of guys."

"No. If you fail—"

"Will you listen to yourself?"

"You don't know how it is, Vince."

"Tell me how it is," Six said, his voice rising, "so I can understand why you're acting like a puppet."

"Swanberg is making a play to take over the town."

"How?"

"That kid of his. And his kid's gang. They've been raising money, pulling scores, and now they're on the edge of starting up a drug operation."

"Really?"

"Once I'm out of the way, the kid can fill the void. Swanberg acts like an advisor or something. He'll pull it off, too. I've never known Swanberg to fail."

"As long as there's somebody to bribe or kill to get to the top, sure," Six said. "I'd like to see him try it on his own."

"He'll show his profits to New York," Giordana said, "and getting rid of me will be forgiven, as long as he's bringing in money."

"You expect him to expose the killing at some point?"

"I don't know what to expect."

"That's why we have to hit the bastard first, Ben. I can't believe I'm the one telling you this."

"You don't have a kid to think about."

"No, I don't," Six agreed. "I also don't have a kid to cloud my judgment."

Giordana turned his head to look at Six. His face was blank. Six couldn't interpret any of the other man's thoughts.

"It's not just Chloe, is it?" Six said.

"That stranger," Giordana said.

"He might be able to help us."

"He's going to fan the flames from cold to hot, Vince. I'm going to lose everything because of him. And that girl they killed."

"What's the story there?"

"Part of the drug operation. She found out about it and threatened to talk. They killed her and her boyfriend, to keep them quiet. Nobody was supposed to come looking for that girl, Vince."

"Well, somebody did, and now we have to deal with the situation in a new way."

"Shooting up Swanberg's place isn't my idea of a smart strategy, Vince."

"Let me do this," Six said. "We gotta take the heat off. I'll find the stranger and get him involved, too. Then we'll find your granddaughter and make it right with Chloe."

"I don't know if there's any way to fix me and Chloe."

"We need to try. We need to try both things."

Ben Giordana nodded. "Start working on a plan, Vince."

Six smiled and rose from the chair. "Yes, sir."

Carl Boskowictz swallowed the last mouthful of scotch and set the glass on the end table beside the couch.

Only the adjustable lamp over his shoulder was on. Darkness bathed the rest of the small living room in his equally small apartment. He'd been off work for a few hours and sat staring at the television. He hated most of what was on TV, so he left the sound off and stared at the images displayed. He wore old jeans and an old shirt, and his gray hair was no longer slicked back, following his after-work shower. His belly bulge was more prominent without his bulletproof vest.

The apartment had an awful feeling of loneliness to it. Boskowictz had no family; his wife had died years earlier of breast cancer. He was alone in the world except for his pals on the force and his street connections. The bad element. Guys like Ben Giordana and Kurt Swanberg.

He hadn't set out to engage in corruption, but it had been the only way to create a nest egg, should one live so long to enjoy such a nest egg. He only had to bide his time until retirement. That wasn't too far away, and then he could get out of Twin Falls and go live wherever he wanted.

He had his mind set on Florida. He'd be a rich old man who hung out on the beach and enjoyed the signs of life all around.

It was an idea, anyway.

He blankly watched the sitcom on the television with no comprehension of what was happening, but the people on the screen seemed deeply involved in the issue. There were a lot of fast cuts and odd reactions, which Bosko-wictz assumed made room for the laugh track. If a show needed a laugh track, he had always said, it wasn't funny.

The phone rang.

Boskowictz had an old-fashioned touchtone on the

table beside the couch, the cord running into the wall behind him. He lifted the receiver and hoped he didn't sound drunk.

"Yeah?"

He sounded drunk. Two scotches and no dinner would do that to you.

The person on the other end of the line didn't care.

"It's me."

"Yes, sir, Mr. Swanberg."

"I'm disappointed that you haven't been able to control the situation."

"It's fluid, sir."

"It's as simple as swatting a fly, Sergeant. If you and Giordana can't handle it, I have people who will."

The line clicked in Boskowictz's ear.

He set the phone down.

His pulse pounded in his head.

"Oh, no," he said to no one.

CHAPTER THIRTY-SEVEN

Stiletto stood at the far end of the parking lot of his hotel, smoking an H. Upmann and watching the passing traffic on Highway 93 about fifteen yards away. It made for a time of peaceful reflection while Stiletto puffed on his cigar. It was warm out, around seventy-three degrees. The light wind was luckily not enough to make lighting or smoking his stogie tough. Lighters didn't like wind, and neither did lit cigars. Blasts of wind tended to make cigars burn improperly, which ruined the flavor. Nothing upset Stiletto more than a ruined cigar when he was trying to relax.

Watching the cars reminded Stiletto of his teenage years when his father, the ever-moving Army officer, took the family to California for a posting in Monterey in the early Nineties. He often hiked off-base late at night and made his way to a particular spot overlooking the ocean, which appeared black at night. Against the dark sky, Scott felt like he was staring into a void. He could hear the waves crashing on the sand, but there was nothing visible in the dark abyss before him. Instead of instilling fear, the view had allowed Scott to turn on the creative side of his brain. In those moments, he'd draw in his sketchbook by the light of the moon, and it didn't matter if the drawings came out as imagined or slightly askew. He was in the zone, and that was where he felt most at peace.

The highway might provide an entirely different view, with the bright headlamps and taillights flashing in front of him and the tall lamps along either side of the highway providing extra illumination, but it put Stiletto in the same frame of mind. Here he could let his thoughts drift, circle back to earlier conversations, and try to sort out the mess he found himself dealing with in Twin Falls, Idaho.

But his mind didn't focus, probably because he simply needed a time out. A break from the situation. A moment away from comparing Shelly Pierce to his daughter, Felicia, which was apt to make him less than his usual stable self. The last thing he needed was to get angry. Scott had killed a lot of men in his career, some in cold blood, but never when angry. Always controlled, calculated, efficient. Such an approach had helped him excel at the CIA. Emotions had no place in combat, even when enemy bullets killed a friend. Revenge certainly had its place, but never when his blood was boiling.

Stiletto puffed on the cigar some more, then turned and started walking. He left the cars and the bright lights behind him and headed past the hotel up Harrison Street, where there were fewer buildings and more open spaces. He wasn't far from the Snake River, and the open lots ahead seemed massive. The lack of light was also welcoming. He was walking into the void he'd once stared into, with the fading sound of speeding cars almost mimicking that of the Pacific Ocean on the Monterey coast.

It was a welcome sound, and Stiletto stopped where Harrison ended and looked into an open field.

That was when the other sound reached him.

A whisper in the night.

Stiletto dove into the dirt with his hands in front of him, landing on the soft ground and rolling right as automatic weapons fire erupted from behind, the slugs kicking up geysers of dirt. Scott kept rolling as the ground started to slope. Then he stopped, rolled again to face the direction of the incoming fire, and pulled the .45 from the shoulder harness under his left arm.

There was movement against the backdrop of the night. Across the lot, emerging from a line of trees, three gunmen ran toward him. Each cradled an automatic rifle. The open field offered no cover. The only way to win was to rush headlong into the fire.

Stiletto rose onto his right knee, using his left for balance as he steadied the .45. He fired twice. The gunman in the center tumbled and fell. The others opened fire as Stiletto rolled left before jumping up and charging ahead. The .45 spat in his extended right arm as the two shooters spread out. The strategy wouldn't be helpful if they caught him in a crossfire, but Stiletto wanted them apart so he had a chance to deal with one target at a time, using the night to his advantage.

Had these shooters been watching him while he observed traffic? It seemed like they should have taken the opportunity to kill him when his back faced their guns, but he also understood the professional's desire to take out a target while avoiding potential risks such as witnesses and cops. Not that the cops would be any hindrance in this town, Stiletto decided as he slapped a fresh magazine into the Colt and triggered a double-tap at one of the shooters. The .45 ACP slugs struck the gunman high in the chest, punching through flesh and bone below the neck. The gunman's strangled cry stretched across the field.

Stiletto dropped and rolled. Not because of incoming rounds, but to confuse the last shooter, whom he couldn't see, which meant the gunman had managed to blend into the darkness and presently had the edge.

The next burst from the gunman came across Stiletto's front from the right. Stiletto swung the .45 in that direction and fired twice, spacing out the rounds. Nobody screamed. He'd seen no muzzle flash, either. He moved his head back and forth, hoping to catch a hint of movement in his peripheral vision. When he did, the last shooter was moving right to left. Stiletto fired and missed and the gunman flattened on the ground, but now Scott had a fix. That was all he needed.

His challenge was directly behind him, however. The

lights of the city. They would expose his silhouette and give the shooter a better target.

It was a risk Stiletto needed to take because if killers were coming after him, they'd be paying Detective Erin Keene a visit as well.

CHAPTER THIRTY-EIGHT

Scott dug his shoes into the dirt and propelled himself forward, the .45 jumping in his right hand as he ran left in a wide arc, reloading as he turned right and zeroed on the last known spot of the gunman. The killer's automatic weapon crackled, Scott wincing as bullets zipped by, and when the shooter stopped, Scott knew he had a dark backdrop at his six o'clock once again.

He ran forward.

The gunman jumped up and ran forward as well.

The two collided, breath rushing out of Stiletto as the hot barrel of the killer's automatic weapon punched his stomach. Scott started to fall, the .45 slipping from his grasp. He grabbed the barrel of the rifle as he went down, kicking the shooter's left leg out from under him at the same time. Both men tipped over and landed in the dirt.

The gunman wore no mask and Stiletto finally saw his face, the man's hair flopping around as he struggled to get back to his feet. Scott was clutching the automatic rifle in both hands. The gunman let go of the rifle to draw back a fist, and that was when Stiletto struck, shoving the rifle into the gunman's chest so hard the force of the blow knocked the wind out of the killer.

Scott grabbed a fistful of dirt and tossed it into the killer's face, then went for his neck as the killer tried to clear the dirt from his eyes. The pair went down again, Scott on top this time, squeezing hard. The gunman flailed at him, but Scott's crushing grip never let up, as if he was trying to shove the man's neck several inches into the dirt.

Only after the gunman finally stopped fighting, and then stopped moving, did Stiletto let up. He staggered away, breathless, snatching up the .45 to shove his last magazine into the grip and stow the pistol beneath his left arm.

There was no time to waste.

He was winded and needed a break but Erin might need help. He felt in his jacket pocket for his cell phone. He dialed her phone, but she didn't pick up.

He still had his car keys, though, in the left pocket of his jeans.

Stiletto started running back down Harrison, his mind on the parking lot where he'd left the rental. He had to get to Erin and fast.

Erin Keene was sleeping fitfully. She kept waking up to look at the alarm clock on the nightstand, the big numbers informing her that perhaps twenty or thirty minutes had passed since the last time she checked the clock.

When she rolled over to look and the clock was blank, she bolted from the bed and grabbed the Glock next to the alarm.

She crouched beside the bed with the familiar gun in both hands. Her hallway nightlight was out, too. The power had been cut.

A noise came from farther down the hall. A clatter. Something had been knocked over. Erin decided that while her Glock was fine, the shotgun in the closet would be better. Keeping the pistol in her right hand, she started for the closet. Then glass shattered and she spun. The glass formerly contained within the frame of the sliding doors leading to her back patio cascaded onto the carpet, the outside light reflecting off the shards like winking stars. A black-clad assassin raised a pistol aimed at her, but she let the Glock do her talking before the man fired.

She worked the trigger in quick strokes, the 9mm kicking back as she fired one round after another. The killer jerked as he entered the room, then fell hard on the glass. The smear of blood from the open wounds on his chest attracted the broken glass, smaller fragments clinging to his shirt as he tried to rise and lift his gun. Erin fired one last round, splitting the man's head down the middle.

Someone yelled down the hall. More shooters. She dropped the empty Glock and opened one closet door, reaching in for the Mossberg 500 clamped to the wall behind some dresses. The magazine tube was full, and she had a carrier attached to the shoulder stock with four more shells inside.

She braced the shotgun against her right shoulder and held the weapon up with her firing hand as she carefully stepped back to the bed, wincing as her bare feet landed on shards of glass. She used her left hand to lift the handset of her nightstand telephone, then let it fall on the floor. There was no dial tone. Her phone line had been cut outside.

She was going to reach for the cell phone beside the landline when something brushed against the hallway wall outside the bedroom.

She didn't wait for a target. She brought her left hand up to support the Mossberg and squeezed the trigger. The shotgun kicked hard but the blast traveled in the right direction, and somebody screamed and thudded against the hallway wall. A man started shouting. Erin pumped the shotgun as she approached the doorway, firing again, and the screaming stopped. Pumping it once more, she raised her aim slightly to reach the far end of the hall. Return fire flashed, two brief pinpoints of light, and a burning sensation filled her stomach. She fired again anyway, then a third shot kicked her left leg out from under her, and she collapsed on the carpet.

She couldn't fire the Mossberg again without pumping the action. She reached for the trombone with her left hand, tugging the shotgun closer to her to get a grip, and then a figure loomed in the darkened hallway ahead. The killer jumped over the body of his comrade and leveled a pistol in her face.

The last thing she saw was the flash from the barrel.

CHAPTER THIRTY-NINE

Stiletto pulled over when he saw the flashing lights.

His hands tightened on the steering wheel. Observers lined the street, most in bathrobes, while squad cars and an ambulance sat in front of Erin's home. The strobing cherry lights filled the dark street and the interior of the car with flashes of red.

The engine idled; Stiletto's hands didn't leave the wheel. There was nothing he could do. Erin had either survived or she hadn't, and he'd hear in due course. Putting the car in gear, he U-turned out of there, his lips in a flat line and his jaw tight all the way back to his hotel.

Police had not yet converged on the open field as he parked the car and returned to his room, where he had a hard time getting to sleep. The longer he tossed and turned, the angrier he became. Perhaps in the past, he'd been able to control his rage in the face of an enemy, but that wouldn't be the case this time. This time, the enemy would feel his wrath. There would be no mercy.

Even if it meant killing Chloe's father.

"My father isn't responsible," she said. "I swear."

"How do you know?"

"He's my father. I just know."

"Not good enough, Chloe."

"What are you going to do, then?"

They spoke quietly but intently in the rear corner booth of the diner as the breakfast crowd filled the seats.

"I'm starting with the band of hoods doing all the dirty work, and we'll see what they say about who's pulling the strings."

"Let me try something first."

"What?"

"I'll confront him. Get him to tell me to my face if he ordered Erin's murder."

The detective's killing was front-page news and the top story on television. Three men had entered Erin Keene's home. She had killed two of them, which meant a third was still at large. Stiletto wondered if he'd meet the man. He wondered if the killer would be among the corpses he planned to leave behind in Twin Falls.

"He'll let you into his place?"

"He's my father."

Stiletto sipped his tea. She kept repeating the words. She wanted him to remember. She wanted him to know what his death would do to her, despite their differences.

Stiletto wasn't sure he could make any promises to her. He didn't try.

"What are you doing here?"

Carl Boskowictz winced as Vince Six asked the question. He stood in the atrium of the Giordana penthouse, a guard on either side of the door, Vince Six standing between them.

"I still work for Ben."

"You two-faced—"

Six took a step forward, but one of the guards grabbed his left arm. "Not here."

Six shook off the grip and stopped but didn't take his eyes off Boskowictz. "I suppose the sooner you see him, the sooner you'll leave." Six moved out of the way. The police sergeant stepped through into the penthouse.

Boskowictz headed for the balcony, where he knew Ben Giordana would be sitting with his morning coffee. He found the boss there dressed in slacks and a dress shirt with the top button undone. The newspaper rested in his lap.

"Can we talk, Ben?"

"Sit."

Boskowictz pulled over a chair and sat with his knees on his elbows.

"Swanberg called me," Boskowictz said, "and told me he was sending people to kill Erin Keene and your daughter's friend. This is something new, Ben. If Swanberg is starting to do more than sit tight, maybe we need to start looking at options."

Ben Giordana punched Boskowictz in the jaw, and the police sergeant tumbled from the chair onto the balcony floor. Six ran to the balcony. Giordana held up a hand and Six relaxed. Boskowictz pushed to his hands and knees, breathing hard. He stayed there.

"I have to admire your survival instinct, Carl," Giordana said, "but I'm afraid that's as far as my thoughts of you go. I think you're right in that Swanberg is planning something. Maybe a takeover. Maybe he wants to get rid of all of us, and we can't have that. I've spoken to New York, and they are not interested in new players taking over the territory. That gives us free rein to take him out."

Boskowictz coughed.

"Stand up, you fat bastard," Giordana ordered.

Carl Boskowictz stood but made no move to sit down again. Vince Six, still in the balcony doorway, stared at him with his arms folded.

"I want to know about security at Swanberg's home," Giordana said. "He has some things in a private safe that I require before we do anything else."

"I'm going up there tonight," the sergeant said. "I can make some notes."

"You know what's going to happen if you tell him I asked about his security, Carl?"

"I don't have to guess."

"You won't live another day if something happens

to me after your chat with Swanberg, which means you better hope I don't have a heart attack or die in my sleep from natural causes. Your killer won't care about the difference."

Boskowictz glanced at Six.

Vince smiled.

Boskowictz looked back at Giordana. "I'll give you the layout."

"Did they hit Chloe's friend?" Giordana said.

"They missed. We found three bodies not far from his hotel. They shot it out in a dirt field. He killed all three."

Giordana nodded. "Get lost, Carl."

The sergeant didn't argue. He pushed past Six and left the penthouse.

"Vince."

Six left the doorway and sat in the chair vacated by Boskowictz.

He said, "We can compare his information to what Tim Dell has already given us to make sure neither are lying."

"And if they're different?"

"Punt."

Six laughed.

"Find Chloe's friend," Giordana said, "and have a chat with him. Let's get him on our side before he torches the whole city. I have a feeling he won't stop to pay attention to who might be in the crossfire."

"Especially you."

"Yeah, especially me."

CHAPTER FORTY

Stiletto finished his tea and asked Chloe to take a walk with him. He had an idea. She told her crew she'd be back in a bit, and they stepped outside and started walking. Street traffic was heavy, but there weren't a lot of pedestrians. Chloe laughed when she realized she still wore her apron. Instead of taking it back in, she removed it and carried it bundled up under her arm.

Chloe took a deep breath. "Wow, fresh air."

"You could probably use more of it," Stiletto said.

"No kidding."

"May I ask a favor?"

"What?"

"Take me with you to see your father."

"Really? Are you sure?"

"Maybe if I ask nicely, he'll tell me the score. If you're convinced that he didn't kill Shelly and didn't order Erin's murder, he might know who did. Maybe he can help."

And I'll get an up-close look at the dragon's lair in case you're wrong.

He kept his thoughts to himself. He felt bad enough making plans behind her back. Verbalizing them would wreck whatever bridge they had between them.

"We can go see him tonight."

"Why so late?"

"He'll have business stuff all day."

"You mean mob stuff."

"Old habits, Scott."

She smiled weakly at him, and Stiletto returned an equally weak smile. Neither knew which side her father fell on, and they were both afraid to find out.

"Let's take your car," he suggested. "They'll probably recognize it."

"Sure, I—"

A screech of tires cut off her reply, and Scott snapped his head around to see a big car speeding up the street. He reached out with his left hand and pushed at Chloe's back while his right clawed for the .45. From the passenger seat, a man with a cigar in his mouth leaned out with an Uzi, and the chattering of the submachine gun drowned out Chloe's scream as they hit the sidewalk together. On his feet with the .45 extended in one hand, Stiletto triggered three rapid blasts that connected with the car, shattering the back window. The tires screeched again as it turned the corner and Scott lowered the smoking Colt .45, turning to Chloe.

Traffic had ground to a halt. Drivers were straining to see what was happening on the sidewalk, but Stiletto ignored them. Stowing the Colt, he helped Chloe to her feet. The front of her uniform was dirty from the fall and she'd skinned a knee, but she was otherwise unharmed.

"I think," she said between gasps, "we'll go see my father right now."

"Let's get out of here."

Stiletto took her hand.

Chloe inserted a key into the elevator panel and turned. As the doors shut, she pressed the button for the penthouse. The elevator car jerked and started climbing.

"You have a key?" Stiletto asked.

"I used to live at this place," she said. "I kept it in case I ever came back, but this isn't the kind of visit I was hoping for."

The elevator continued its ascent. Chloe watched the floor indicator above the door with wide eyes. She looked small all of a sudden. She looked like a little girl hoping her father would be there when she needed him.

Stiletto didn't check the .45 under his arm. He'd reloaded after the street ambush, but to check the gun now would set the wrong tone. The house guards would want to hold it anyway. Better to be seen surrendering the pistol in the name of a peaceful meeting than to enter the penthouse aggressively.

The doors slid open.

Chloe didn't move. The guards at either side of the door stared back.

Chloe cleared her throat and started forward. She stopped in front of them.

"Tell Mr. Giordana his daughter is here to see him."

"Who's that?" the man on the left of the door said.

"He's with me."

The right-side guard stepped forward, gesturing for Scott to lift his arms. Scott held his arms out perpendicular to the floor and submitted to a full pat-down after telling the guard where to find the Colt .45. The guard removed the gun from the holster, then ejected the magazine and locked back the slide. He placed the Colt on a table behind him.

Announcing that Scott was "clear," the second guard radioed for Six, but before he finished the call, the penthouse doors opened and Vince Six surveyed the guests.

"Chloe," he said.

"Hello, Vince."

"This is a surprise."

"We need to see my father. Now."

"Sure. Who's your friend?"

"Stiletto," he said. "Scott Stiletto. We need to see Giordana."

"We were going to come see you in a bit," Six told him. "Saves us the trouble. Come in."

Chloe stormed past Six into the penthouse. Stiletto let

Vince stand aside before he entered. The enforcer closed the door.

Ben Giordana came in from the balcony.

"Chloe—"

"Not a word, you son of a bitch!"

She planted her feet on the carpet halfway to the balcony. Stiletto and Six stopped and hung back.

Giordana, flustered, tried to say more, but Chloe's words bulldozed over anything he might have said.

"Did you send people to kill Erin Keene? Did you send people to kill Scott on the street and almost kill me?"

"Chloe—"

"Yes or no, Daddy. That's all I want to hear out of you!"

Ben Giordana's face blanched. He blinked.

Then he said, "No."

CHAPTER FORTY-ONE

"What happened?"

Chloe put her hands on her hips. All her attention was focused on her father. She explained the drive-by assassination attempt and how Scott had shot at the car as it left the scene.

"Vince, check it out," Giordana said.

Six crossed to another room and closed the door.

"It wasn't me, Chloe," he said.

"Then who?"

"Swanberg."

"Who the hell is Swanberg?"

Scott touched Chloe's elbow. She snapped her attention to him, and Scott's first instinct was to get ready to block a slap. She seemed primed for a strike but didn't lift her hand.

"Let's hear him out," Stiletto said. To Giordana, "You got any whiskey?"

"I got a lot of whiskey," Giordana said. "Come outside and join me."

Stiletto accepted the Makers and Coke Giordana poured.
Chloe had no interest in the stunning view the balcony
provided. She sat with her back to the balcony wall, arms
folded, her face tight in a scowl. Scott sat opposite her,
next to Giordana, and gazed in the direction of the Snake
River.

"Not a bad view," he said.

"It helps pass the time," Giordana said. "Mr. Stiletto—"

"Call me Scott."

"I'm going to tell you a story, Scott, and it will explain
why you're here, and what you need to do."

"You seem to know a lot about me."

"I know nothing about you. I do know what you're
doing. And why."

"Go ahead." Stiletto sipped his drink.

"I'm in charge of the Outfit here in Twin Falls," Giordana said. "I answer to the New York Commission. I'm
sure there are many other things Chloe has told you, so I
don't need to say much more than that. However, what
you don't know, and what I'm going to tell you now will
show you that I'm somebody who is caught between a
rock and a hard place."

Chloe scoffed. "This should be interesting."

Giordana ignored his daughter. He told the story of
how he joined the Outfit and how they ordered him to

commit a homicide to cement his position in their ranks. He told, also, of how Kurt Swanberg had obtained concrete evidence of the murder, and now held that evidence over his head to make sure he did what Swanberg wanted, when he wanted it, no matter what. Those "favors" had included, Giordana explained, helping to cover up the murders of Shelly Pierce and Chad Mendoza.

"Cover-up?" Stiletto said.

"My people didn't kill her," Giordana said. "Swanberg doesn't have the infrastructure I have in this city. I could block the cops from getting too far and I could intimidate the witnesses, all that. But I only did it because Swanberg ordered me too. As you know, there's no statute of limitations on murder."

Stiletto glanced at Chloe. The scowl hadn't left her face. Perhaps this wasn't news to her. He suddenly hurt for her. It was one thing to know your father was a Mafioso; it was another thing to know he was a killer, too. But maybe she already knew that. Maybe that was all it took to keep her away from him. Maybe he saw a little of his own daughter in Chloe. Maybe their reactions were the same.

"Who killed Shelly?" Stiletto said.

"Swanberg's son, Damien."

"Why did Swanberg's son kill Shelly?"

"Swanberg is getting into the drug business, and he's using his kid as the conduit," Giordana said. "Swanberg wants to push me out and let his kid take over, and run the operation from the shadows. Damien will only be a figurehead."

"Tell me more."

"There's a third party they need to get rid of. Problem is, this third party is the one with the cartel connection. Damien can't do anything until he's out of the way and Damien establishes the connection in his place."

"Who is this third party?"

"Roger Ivy. He—"

"Runs a nightclub," Stiletto said. "We've already met. Shelly thought his son, Peter, might replace Chad."

"Yeah, well, Shelly had no idea what she was getting into."

"Did she find out about the drugs through Peter?"

"I'm not exactly sure," Giordana said. "I think she found out via Chad, who was working with Damien. Well, she raised hell. I think it was the first time she realized how Chad earned his money because she didn't seem to notice, or care about, their activities prior to that."

"Did she go to the cops?"

"She didn't get that far. Damien shot her and Chad before they could."

"How do they plan to get Roger Ivy to turn over the cartel connection?" Stiletto said. His drink was almost gone.

"That I'm not sure," Giordana said. "They've made no overt moves yet."

"The jewelry heist—"

"Was a big one, and they've already spent the money."

"How?"

"They've hired four shooters," Giordana said. "We know what hotel they're staying at, but I have no idea what they're going to be used for."

"Sounds like I need to go back to the loft."

"I was also hoping," Giordana said, "you might help us with another matter too."

"Which is what?"

Before Giordana could explain, Six came out onto the balcony.

CHAPTER FORTY-TWO

"Those new shooters the Swanberg kid brought in?" Six said. "I think they're the ones who took a shot at Chloe and, um—"

"Scott."

"Yeah."

"Where are they?"

"Not sure, but none of them were hurt."

"Bad aim, I guess," Stiletto said.

"Sit down, Six."

Vince Six found a chair inside and sat in the doorway while his boss and Scott continued.

"I was about to tell Mr. Stiletto," Giordana said, "about your idea of raiding Swanberg's place."

"Uh-huh."

"What's in Swanberg's place?" Stiletto said.

"Evidence."

"The evidence against you?"

"Exactly."

Chloe scoffed.

"You want me to help you recover it?"

"We'll take away Swanberg's hold if we can get it," Giordana said. "It will make our job easier."

Stiletto laughed so hard he slapped his right leg. "That's rich. No. Absolutely not. Our alliance, or whatever this is, doesn't go as far as me helping you recover evidence of somebody you killed so you can destroy it once and for all. I appreciate the tip on the drug operation, though."

Six jumped in. "And what exactly do you think will happen once you shoot Swanberg's kid? If we don't get that material now, we'll get it later."

"It will be better then. What makes you think you can pull off a raid on Swanberg's place?"

"Insiders," Six said. "We have two people feeding us information on where the safe is and all that."

"Nuts."

"Why?"

"Several reasons. If you go in there, you need as many men as he has for security, and somebody's going to talk. While you're there, you might as well whack Swanberg and finish the whole thing. But what if he has a dead man's switch? If he goes, the evidence you're trying to recover might go out anyway. For sure, he has more than one copy."

Stiletto stopped speaking to let the words sink in. Six and Giordana were too emotionally invested in the issue to clearly see the problems. He didn't think they were stupid.

Giordana turned to Six. "Thoughts?"

Six cursed and shook his head. "He's right."

"What do we do?"

"Tim Dell and Boskowictz will find out what we asked them to learn. We will file that information away for the worst-case scenario."

Stiletto said, "Now you're talking."

"What is the worst-case scenario?" Giordana said.

"Say I fail," Stiletto said, "and Swanberg's kid gets what he wants, and the whole thing blows up. You'll need to go for the throat at that time, and whatever intelligence you have will come in handy."

"Maybe," Six added.

"Sure."

"Meaning what?"

"Meaning all kinds of things, Ben," Stiletto said. "We're not talking exact science."

Stiletto finished his drink and set the glass down.

"I'm sticking with Damien and the gang," Scott said. "Don't get in my way."

Stiletto rose from his seat. Chloe left her chair, as well.

"Stay out of ours," Giordana said.

"Shouldn't be too hard."

"Hey," Six said.

Stiletto faced the enforcer.

"What kind of weapons do you have?"

"My pistol."

"You'll need more than that." Six glanced at Giordana. Giordana waved a hand.

Six took out his wallet, removed a business card, and used a pen from another pocket to scribble a number on the back. He handed the card to Stiletto, who frowned.

"I'm renting a car," he said, "I don't need a mechanic."

"Go there and tell them I sent you. My cell is on the back in case they need to reach me."

"Sure." Stiletto slipped the card into his back pocket.

Scott started across the penthouse, with Chloe beside him. The guard handed back Stiletto's gun and held the elevator door open.

Stiletto didn't force a conversation as he and Chloe drove back to the diner. Traffic flowed smoothly enough that they wouldn't be in the car long anyway.

At least he had answers now. He knew why Shelly Pierce had been murdered, and he knew that Roger Ivy had indeed played a role. Indirect, maybe, but his cartel connection made him equally responsible, even if it had been Damien Swanberg who had pulled the trigger.

Now Scott had to figure out his next move. If Damien and his gang were planning an operation against Ivy, it might make sense to let them carry it out. Even the playing field a bit. Keep them focused on Ivy while he sniped them from behind.

But they had shooters, Giordana had said. Four of them. He wasn't too impressed with them after the drive-by, but it was very difficult to hit anybody from a moving car.

What forces did Ivy have on his side? Or was he on his own?

Not much longer now.

Chloe sat staring out the windshield with her arms folded.

"Are you okay?" Stiletto said.

"My father didn't bother to ask me that."

"That's not what I meant."

"It's only a skinned knee."

"That's not what I meant, either."

"I'm fine."

"Really?"

"No."

"What's bothering you?"

"You're like them. Exactly like them."

"Exactly how? I recall telling your father to kick rocks over the Swanberg raid."

"You're a killer, too."

"Yeah," Stiletto said. "I suppose we're alike in some ways."

"This is insane. I'm living in an insane asylum."

"The world is insane, Chloe. People like me are trying to make it less so, and people like Erin Keene, but it's an uphill battle because of people like your father."

Chloe smoothed the skirt of her uniform.

"Look at it this way," Stiletto said. "Your father is off my suspect list."

"That's a relief."

"I suspect you truly are relieved," Stiletto said. "I know the conflict with your father won't be solved easily, but you know you were afraid he was the one."

"I know."

"And Chloe? I've never killed anybody who didn't deserve it."

His hands tightened on the wheel.

And I'm going to enjoy killing Damien Swanberg.

Stiletto dropped Chloe at the diner, and she didn't say good-bye. Stiletto pulled back into traffic and left her to herself. He had more important matters on his mind. He was within reach of concluding his time in Twin Falls, but his actions needed to be timed perfectly.

He staked out the loft once again, knowing Damien and Armstrong were inside because their cars were parked in back of the Shipwreck Bar. When they left in Damien's Challenger, Stiletto followed. They visited a hardware store and exited pushing a cart, then loaded the items into the Challenger's trunk. He stayed with them for a drive north to the far end of town closest to the Snake River. They stopped at a cabin that enjoyed a view of the river while being surrounded by trees. Scott used binoculars to get a better look after parking well away from the location. He figured the cabin was the "hideout" referred to by Peter Ivy.

The surrounding trees made it difficult to see every-thing going on, but Damien and Armstrong unloaded their hardware store items inside, then thundered away in the Challenger. Stiletto exited his rental and hiked the distance to the cabin. He started sweating right away. The temperature was pushing a hundred degrees and the coat concealing the Colt .45 needed to go, fast, but Scott had no other option.

He reached the trees near the cabin. Observing through them, he saw no signs of life inside and no sentries. If the hired shooters weren't at their hotel, like Vince Six believed, they also weren't at this location.

Removing the .45 from his holster, he approached the house from the side. Curtains covered the windows. Sti-letto approached one and tried to see through the gaps, but like before, nothing indicated anybody was inside.

Scott put away his gun and walked around the side to the porch. At the front door, he used his lock picks to unlock the knob lock and snap back the deadbolt. The .45 out again, he stepped inside.

The front room was bare, boxes spread about, the hard-ware stores purchases remaining in their shopping bags and placed in a corner.

The next room was in the process of being set up with cots, with a refrigerator—empty, Stiletto discovered—plugged in and running.

Down the hall, Stiletto checked three empty bedrooms. At the far end of the hall in the master bedroom, he discovered a steel cage complete with restraints. The cage looked to be six by six, large enough for a person of medium height to be kept within the bars.

Frowning, he put away the gun.

Damien and his gang were planning to kidnap somebody and hold them at the cabin, using their newly-hired shooters as guards.

And Stiletto figured he knew the intended victim.

CHAPTER FORTY-THREE

Carl Boskowictz drove south out of the city and into the flat country, where it seemed civilization had decided not to stop. A lot of open fields and farming operations, plus scattered homes here and there. He drove by all that. After the hot day, it was nice to have the windows open and feel the cooler air rush into the car. Boskowictz knew these would be the last comfortable moments before some very uncomfortable ones spent in the presence of Kurt Swanberg.

He was a bundle of nerves and had been so since the phone call from Swanberg, where he stated his own people would handle the Erin Keene and "mystery man" problems. The result? Mystery man still lived, Erin Keene was dead, and Boskowictz found himself on the wrong end of the boss's scheme. He knew now that Swanberg had kicked off the killing spree, and that anybody connected to Ben Giordana, even a go-between like him, would be wiped out without a thought as Swanberg and that stupid kid of his solidified their positions and sought the blessing of the New York Commission.

His survival instinct, as Giordana had called it, had made him return to the hand that had once fed him and try to get back into Ben's good graces, but he should have expected Giordana's wrath. He was lucky all Ben had done was smack him once, although he was fairly sure Giordana wouldn't order a shooting in the penthouse. The only thing keeping him alive right now, and no mistake, was that Giordana and Six needed him to provide information on Swanberg's security arrangements.

After that, the possibility exited that Giordana would throw Boskowictz to the wolves.

The truth was, Boskowictz was a coward. He liked the status quo. Giordana ran the rackets, and Boskowictz hung around to help with problems and kept Swanberg happy, too. There was no need for killing, and they'd all gotten along, despite the tension between Giordana and Swanberg, for years. No problem. Now, Swanberg had changed all that. His craving for power had changed the pattern. Why? He was already rich. What else did he need? But those questions ignored what the police sergeant was really thinking. He realized he wasn't the tough guy he'd thought he was.

But if he juggled carefully, Boskowictz figured he might make it out of Twin Falls alive after all.

As he drove, the car's engine lulled him into a calmer mood.

A half-hour later, he was escorted into Kurt Swanberg's dining room, where the elder Swanberg was finishing his meal, but no place had been set for Boskowictz.

"Take a seat, Carl," Swanberg said as he shoved a piece of steak into his mouth.

Swanberg was a big man. His weight reflected his prosperity and his now-sedentary life. As he'd told the press once in an interview, he'd worked his tail off for decades, and now it was time to take it easy and enjoy the results.

Boskowictz sat near Swanberg. The butler placed a glass of ice water in front of the police sergeant.

Swanberg wasn't a horrible host, after all.

"What do the kids say today?" Swanberg said as he wiped his mouth. He had white hair and a white goatee and wore a white suit. Lines and wrinkles had replaced the youthful, boyish looks that had helped him score so well with the ladies.

The walls of the dining room were not white. The dining room resembled a hunting lodge, with a lot of wood and logs and stuffed and mounted animals.

"What about, Mr. Swanberg?"

"You know, that whole 'sorry, not sorry' line or whatever it is? I heard Damien say it once."

"Can't say I'm familiar."

"No matter. Anyway, I'm sorry, not sorry that I've

had to escalate things, Carl. It's necessary. My kid and I, we're doing things, moving and shaking, all that. We're going to get rid of Giordana and make Twin Falls the envy of the Outfit, get it?"

"Sure."

"What's the problem?"

"If you're starting fresh, I might be on the chopping block."

"Oh, come on, do you think I'm mad? We had to get rid of that cop. I wish we could get rid of that other guy. I'm not going to get rid of you. In fact, I see plenty of opportunity for you, Carl."

"Doing what?"

"We'll decide that later. What I need from you most is for you to, you know, behave yourself. Stay cool. Do the kids still say that?"

"I think 'stay cool' is more what we used to say at their age."

"You're right. I like the way it sounds. Especially in this heat." Swanberg laughed. "I've had enough of this." Swanberg pushed away his plate, and the butler quickly collected the dish. "Let's go to my office and have a drink."

Swanberg led Boskowictz down a brightly lit hallway with various antique decorations displayed along the walls but no paintings. Swanberg didn't care for painted art. He liked tangible items he could pick up and examine in detail.

In the den at the end of the hall, Swanberg flicked a switch and lights shone on the desk to their left. The desk and a set of chairs sat near a wall. In the middle of the wall, in a place others would have covered with a painting, but not Kurt Swanberg, was the glossy steel front of a wall safe.

Another sitting area with couches and chairs remained in darkness. Swanberg told Boskowictz to sit down again while he poured two glasses of Scotch. He handed one to the police sergeant and eased into his chair.

With the light shining above and the rest of the room in black, Boskowictz suddenly realized how thousands of suspects put under the "hot lights" at the police station felt. He had a big fat bullseye on his chest. Who did Swanberg think he was kidding? He wanted Boskowictz to behave, all right. He wanted Boskowictz to stay away from Giordana until the finishing kill. Boskowictz had to decide if he was going to go with Swanberg and deal with the upheaval of the "transition," should he even survive, or throw his line back in with Giordana and the eventual return to status quo.

"You gonna drink any of that, Carl?"

Startled, Boskowictz covered his nervousness with a sip of Johnny Walker.

"I don't give that scotch to just anybody, you know," Swanberg said, laughing, his belly moving up and down like Santa Claus—if Santa Claus was preparing to unleash murder and mayhem on an unsuspecting population.

CHAPTER FORTY-FOUR

It was the crudest possible set-up.

As Swanberg continued to talk about the future, he said he wanted to give Boskowictz a down payment on that future, and rose from his desk to open the wall safe without any concealment of the combination. Boskowictz watched the man's fat fingers roll the knob left, right, left, vigorously yanking the door open. Inside, over Swanberg's shoulder, Boskowictz saw stacks of money and leather-bound books.

When he turned around, he was holding one of the stacks of cash.

"It's going to be you and me, Carl, and my kid, running this town." Swanberg counted out three bills, hesitated, and added two more. "There you go. That'll keep you in groceries for a few months."

Boskowictz collected the money from the desktop without looking at the bills. He folded them into his shirt pocket.

Swanberg showed the police sergeant out, chatting away as he did, but the words were lost on Boskowictz. There was thunder in his head, a nervous pulse-beat. He wanted to run for cover, but he had to pretend that feeling didn't exist.

When he finally pulled away from Swanberg's house, he let out a big sigh of relief.

Driving back to the city, he went over the information he had managed to jam into his mind. At least six guards, and the combination to the safe. He figured the leather-bound books were what Giordana would require. He'd pass along the info to Vince Six and let the big enforcer decide what to do from there.

One thing was for sure.

If Swanberg put two and two together after the raid, he'd know Boskowictz had misbehaved, despite his pleas to the contrary.

Which was what the entire meeting had been about. Swanberg was testing him. So was Giordana.

Boskowictz knew who he'd throw his support behind.

Swanberg placed a bookmark in the middle of the hardcover he held and put the book on the coffee table in front of him. He reached for a cup of tea on the table beside the leather couch and sipped.

Now that Boskowictz was gone, he could once again enjoy the solitude his home offered.

He regarded the book, a biography of the pioneers of Silicon Valley in the 1960s and '70s. He'd had a chance to inhabit their world for a period of years, making his fortune in the computer and technology business, and reading the stories of how it all began filled him with the same sense of wonder he'd held when first discovering the magical world of personal computing. He envied the newbies getting into the business. They had a lot to look forward to as they improved upon the foundation built by others.

Now Swanberg had other business interests. He had never been above skullduggery to get what he required, and the connections he had made in California continued to serve him well—especially now that his son, Damien, was becoming more larcenous. Not quite out of control, but he needed direction. Somebody to guide him, and with Ben Giordana in Twin Falls, they could never achieve anything near the goals they had in mind.

Which meant Giordana had to go and Swanberg needed to take his place, and he had to do it the hard way.

The Earl Gray tasted good. Swanberg took another sip and set down the mug.

His brightly lit study contained bulletproof windows. He stood up to stretch, then wandered to one of those windows to look out at the darkness. He should have security lights. His guard troops insisted he have them, but he liked the idea of looking out into a void, a void only he could fill with whatever he dreamed of next. Once one stops dreaming, scheming, reaching for the stars, one begins to atrophy and die.

Swanberg had no intention of dying tonight, or any other night anytime soon.

His stables were out there somewhere. He didn't really care, though. Horses had been a fling, a one-night stand, and when he realized that dealing with live animals didn't hold his attention as much as he would have liked, he had decided not to fill the stables but let others work their equine magic. He could be a spectator. Watching horseracing was a great way to pass the time on a warm Sunday afternoon.

And Twin Falls had certainly been warm enough lately.

Both naturally, and with the kind of heat trouble brings.

Like Chloe Giordana's mystery man.

He had to find the mystery man and soon, and deal with him in such a way that he never made trouble for anybody again.

Damien and his crew would be moving on Peter Ivy within days.

Nothing could stand in the way of his son taking over the Mexican cartel connection. The alliance was vital to their goals.

He wondered how long it would be before Giordana sent somebody, or a group of somebodies, to attack his property to get at the contents of the wall safe. There was no way Boskowictz would resist sharing what he'd witnessed. Swanberg had his troops ready, too. Hiding. In the darkness. Baiting a trap for whoever showed up.

The casket was closed for the funeral.

Stiletto arrived late, well after the memorial service, because even sitting in the back of the room, he feared he might be a distraction to those who knew of him but not quite who he was. As he watched the mourners gather at Erin Keene's gravesite from a distance and partially obscured by a tree, he saw Chloe and others he assumed were from the Justice for Jane group clustered together, a few crying. He sensed a coolness in Chloe. She hadn't contacted him to see if he wanted to attend with her, and he admitted that he hadn't tried to contact her, either. She was at a fork in the road, he knew. Did she throw in with somebody she knew was a killer, who planned to kill a killer, who reminded her of her father, or was she going to remain detached as long as she could?

Stiletto still wore his jacket to cover the Colt .45, but at least the weather was cooler than the day before. It was in the mid-eighties instead of the 100-degree temperatures the day before. Stiletto wanted to laugh. What was the difference, really? But it took his mind off watching the graveside crew lower Erin Keene's casket into the ground. They were burying a good woman, a good cop, a good person. Stiletto made a fist with his left hand and squeezed tight. Her death would not go unavenged. She would not have died in vain. Stiletto was going to make the guilty pay if he had to burn Twin Falls to the ground.

The crowd began to disperse. Stiletto thought he saw

Chloe look in his direction, but if she saw him, she gave no indication. Scott wasn't watching her. His eyes were on Carl Boskowictz, dressed in his formal police uniform, and wiping his eyes with a handkerchief. Are you kidding? What was that snake crying about?

Stiletto drove away from the cemetery and changed gears in his mind. He had to get back on the trail of Damien and his crew. He was going to let them kidnap Peter Ivy. He wanted Roger Ivy loosed up enough to talk and name his cartel connection. Only a gun to his son's head would insure he told the truth. Then Stiletto would go and rescue the kid, though he had no idea why; maybe because he was a father too, but that made his head hurt. By that rationale, he should also spare Kurt Swanberg the pain of killing his son. Of course, Swanberg's pain, whatever it might be, wouldn't last long. Scott was going to kill him, too.

Maybe Chloe was right to stay away. Maybe one killer was the same as another.

Stiletto's grip tightened on the steering wheel and he clenched his jaw.

It was one of those few moments where he wanted to say the heck with it all and let the enemy destroy each other.

But deep down, he knew he'd never walk away.

This was the kind of mission he was good at. While it pained him that he spent more time patching the wounds of victims than preventing them from becoming victims in the first place, he knew the only way to save Twin Falls from itself was to cut out the cancer within with such ferocity that it never returned.

He had his plan.

Stiletto hoped Ben Giordana and Vince Six listened to his counsel to avoid a raid on the Swanberg estate. Not only would the effort fail, but it might also cause a ripple effect that scared off Stiletto's quarry. Maybe it would have been better to team up with Giordana and Six; he might have helped diffuse their emotional involvement in the issue and help them see that strategy was preferable to action at this point.

But he'd made his choice. The chips were going to fall, and he'd have to deal with the result.

CHAPTER FORTY-FIVE

Carl Boskowictz slumped heavily in the corner booth of the busy bar. He was four scotches deep, with no end in sight.

When Scott dropped into the seat across from the police sergeant, Boskowictz bit off a curse.

"Bad day, Sergeant?"

"You punk. This is all your fault."

"My fault?"

"If you hadn't shown up, none of this would be happening."

Stiletto looked at the drunk man for a moment. He might have a point in that Erin Keene would still be alive had Stiletto not stepped into the action, but the Swanberg operation would indeed be happening, whether he was there or not.

"You know that's not entirely true, Sergeant."

"She's dead because of you."

"No, she's dead because of people like you."

"Me?"

"You're corrupt, Boskowictz. You're sitting with the bad guys who are strangling this town and keeping good cops like Erin from doing their jobs."

Boskowictz downed what remained of his drink. A passing waitress asked if he wanted another, but Stiletto told her the police sergeant had consumed enough.

The waitress moved on.

"What's really on your mind tonight, Sergeant?"

"None of this was supposed to happen," Boskowictz Boskowictz said. "We had a good thing going. No trouble. Nobody got killed."

"That's not true. I'm here because two people got killed."

"I mean before that," Boskowictz said. "Swanberg has ruined everything."

"You were a fool to think otherwise, Sergeant."

"I know that now. You'd think after all the crap I've been involved with, I wouldn't be upset about Erin. But I am. I really am."

"What are you looking for, Sergeant?"

"I need a way out."

"Is there one?"

"I passed some info about Swanberg's place to Ben and Six. They told me to kick rocks."

"Uh-huh."

"Ben's pissed at me, and I suppose he has a right. I turned my back on him years ago while pretending I was still on his side. Swanberg isn't going to keep me around after he takes out Ben; there's no way."

"It's hard to live with a target on your back."

"How would you know?"

"Don't ask," Stiletto told him.

"You know why the girl was killed now, right?"

"I have it all. What I want to know is where you truly stand, Sergeant? You have a chance to redeem yourself if you play your cards right."

Boskowictz dropped his eyes to the table. There were droplets of condensation on the surface that had come from his drinks. Either that or he was crying. He wasn't quite sure.

"I have something you can use," Boskowictz said.

"Like what?"

"You aren't wrong. I've been up to my neck in crap for decades," the police sergeant said. "But I kept track of everything. I know where all the bodies are buried. I have a little packet of stuff that can put half the city in the federal penitentiary. And that's the important thing. I give this to you, it's gotta go to the Feds. Not the city, not the state prosecutors. To the Feds. They're the only ones clean enough to handle it."

"Okay," Stiletto said.

"I'm not in good shape to drive," Boskowictz admitted.

"My rental is parked out front," Stiletto said. "Why don't we get your material and you can crash on your couch or something."

"That's a good idea," Boskowictz said.

Boskowictz leaned on Stiletto as they exited the bar and managed to cross the street during a break in traffic. They reached Scott's rental car, and Boskowictz leaned on a fender while Stiletto opened the passenger door. The police sergeant managed to get inside without banging his head. Stiletto dropped behind the wheel and started the car. Boskowictz had already passed out and was snoring. Luckily, he'd told Stiletto how to get to his apartment before they left.

They reached the apartment and the sergeant brought Stiletto up to his domicile. Scott waited while he dug into a cubby in the back of a closet. Scott's hand was never far from the Colt Combat Government in the shoulder holster under his left arm. He didn't suspect Boskowictz of anything untoward, but he wasn't taking any chances, either.

The police sergeant handed Stiletto a thick folder tied closed with twine. He said everything Scott needed was in the stack, and there were further instructions within the folder where to find info Boskowictz had stashed elsewhere. Stiletto took the bundle without knowing what he was going to do with it and left Boskowictz passed out face-down on his bed.

Stiletto drove away with the bundle on the passenger seat. If the information within could cut the cancer out of Twin Falls, great, but it was useless until Scott had wrecked the machine doing all the damage. He had to break the back of Swanberg, his kid, and the kid's gang before the Boskowictz file would be of use. With Swanberg gone, the rest of the rats would have nowhere to go, nowhere to hide, and nobody pulling the strings to keep them out of trouble.

He stowed the bundle in the safe inside his hotel room.

Scott checked his watch. It was getting late, and he needed to hit the road again.

The mission was approaching the climax, and he had to make sure he was there to keep everything on track.

"I'm going to cut him off," Joe Armstrong said.

"No," Damien Swanberg said. "Shove him onto the sidewalk."

"He'll hit a light pole or something."

"I don't care what he hits. We need to get him now."

Damien Swanberg sat in the passenger seat of the stolen four-door Silverado. Joe was behind the wheel of the raised truck, with Teddy Stone and Eric Foster, the fourth member of the team, in the back seat.

Eric Foster, a few days out of the hospital, still looked a little rough from the beating he had taken outside the Shipwreck Bar, but he was ready to get back in the game, and Swanberg was glad to have his squad back to full force. He needed every hand on deck for this job because it was the biggest yet, the one that would let him and his father take over every aspect of criminal activity in Twin Falls and rule the city with an iron fist. And when their power expanded to other states in the Midwest, they'd be unstoppable.

The target car was ahead, passing through an intersection. The stolen truck shook as they went over a bump. Damien balled a fist and clenched his teeth.

"Come on, Joe, hurry."

A surge of power carried the truck forward as it overtook the target car, a compact Ford. The man behind the wheel rode alone. He wasn't much older than Damien and his crew. His own father was part of a criminal network within the city, working with a Mexican cartel on a drug connection. One that had so far remained undercover, but the Swanberg contingent had plans to change that.

The driver of the target car was Peter Ivy.

With a screech of tires, Joe Armstrong pulled in front of Peter Ivy's car and swung right, slamming into the left front fender of the Ford. Tires screeched as the Ford, forced sideways, failed to withstand the push from the big truck. The Ford jolted over the curb onto the sidewalk and stopped instantly as the front end crunched into a light post. The hood flew up and the front bumper smashed inward. Joe stopped the truck in the street.

Other cars stacked up behind them, horns blaring. Damien and his crew jumped out and rushed Peter Ivy's car with drawn guns.

Damien pulled open the Ford's door. Peter Ivy mumbled something, a stunned look on his face from the impact of the airbag. Damien used a sharp knife to slice off Ivy's seatbelt and told Eric to help haul him out.

The two men carried Peter Ivy to the truck, Teddy Stone dropping the tailgate. Damien and Eric tossed Peter Ivy into the truck bed. Teddy jumped in as well and pulled the gate shut while the other two raced back to the cab. Joe hit the gas and the truck surged ahead.

The backed-up traffic started to return to normal, a few people pulling over to call the police.

One motorist in particular paid close attention to the crash and the kidnapping, although he didn't hang around to wait for the cops. Scott Stiletto took the first left out of the area.

CHAPTER FORTY-SIX

The car mechanic had proven useful, indeed.

Stiletto was well aware that "mechanic" in Mafia-speak often meant hitman, but Sharkey's Custom Hot Rods was the real deal, with a work bay full of classic muscle cars and modern sports machines undergoing various levels of surgery for more horsepower or whatever other modifications the owners were seeking.

Sharkey himself assisted Stiletto once he told the lady at the front office that Six had sent him. The weapons were located in a locked room at the end of a dingy hallway with grease-stained walls. Various locked cases were stacked here and there. Stiletto said he had a pistol but needed a long arm and ammunition. Sharkey showed him a pristine Kriss Vector .45 ACP submachine gun, a stubby weapon with a unique buffer system that soaked up actual recoil and reduced muzzle flip to the point where there was virtually none. Since its caliber matched Stiletto's Colt, it made ammunition selection easy. Scott loaded up on the Vector, several extended magazines, and a case of .45 ammo.

Stiletto also bought a set of wire garrotes, along with two flash-bang stun grenades and a Ka-bar knife.

With the Vector fully loaded in the truck of the rental, he set about tracking the movements of Damien Swanberg and his crew, thus witnessing the forced crash of Peter Ivy's Ford and the kidnapping.

From the scene of the crash, Stiletto powered through the streets to the back lot of Club Ivy, where he expected to find Peter's father, Roger.

Back where he had started.

If only he had known at the time how close he'd been to the truth.

Stiletto parked crooked between two other vehicles but didn't take the time to correct. He left the rental and quickly crossed the lot to the rear exit. It was a warm night, and the air conditioning units on the roof rumbled loudly. The A/C units could not cover the music blasting within the club walls, however. Stiletto felt the vibrations of the bass as he stepped through the doorway.

Slipping the .45 from shoulder leather, he tapped the barrel on the open door of Roger Ivy's office. The club owner sat behind his desk, his head bent over paperwork.

"Hey," Scott said.

Ivy looked up sharply. "You—"

"Again, yeah." Stiletto stepped into the office and kicked the door shut. He leaned against it. "This time, we're having a different conversation."

"I don't understand."

"Within the next few minutes, your phone is going to ring. You will be told that your son has been kidnapped and that the kidnappers want something from you. Once you get that call, we can talk further."

Roger Ivy's eyes widened. He took a breath, then said, "Why don't you explain what's going on? And understand that if you hurt my son—"

"I had nothing to do with this, you idiot," Stiletto snapped. "You're dealing with Swanberg. I don't have to explain why."

The color drained from Ivy's face.

"I watched them grab your kid a little bit ago," Stiletto continued. "I've been following Swanberg's kid, Damien. I don't need to explain him either, do I?"

"No."

"You and your son lied to me."

"We didn't tell you the whole story."

"Same thing."

"Well—"

"You're not in a spot to argue, Roger. Keep those hands where I can see them."

"I was just—"

"You freeze right there, or it won't matter what happens to your kid, will it? You won't be around."

"All right, all right. Let's settle down."

"When that phone rings and Damien tells you what he wants, you're going to agree."

"What does he want?"

"Access to your cartel connection. You to get out of the way. Preferably far away, which means you get out of Twin Falls or suddenly get lead poisoning."

Ivy nodded. Stiletto gave him credit for not trying to argue. The club owner knew when the lies wouldn't work any longer.

The walls shook from the music in the club.

"How do you put up with this noise?" Stiletto asked.

"You tune it out after a while."

The desk phone rang.

Roger Ivy jumped as if hit with an electrical shock. He glanced sharply at Stiletto, who gestured to the phone with his gun. Roger Ivy lifted the handset.

The club owner spoke to the party on the other end of the line, displaying the proper shock of a father learning that his son has been kidnapped and will meet a grisly end should the kidnappers' demands not be met. If Roger Ivy had thought Scott was kidding, the words from Damien Swanberg erased that notion. Ivy promised to do whatever he was asked and hung up the phone.

He sat shaking for a few moments.

Stiletto said, "What do they want?"

"Exactly what you said. My cartel contact."

"You knew Shelly was killed because she found out about Damien's plans, didn't you?"

"Yes."

"All right, Roger, this is how it's going to work. Are

you listening? Look at me, Roger."

"I'm listening."

"I know where the gang is hiding, and I'm going to go get your kid. When I bring him back, you will give me the name of your cartel contact, and any other information you think I need to have. If you try to pull a fast one, I'll kill you both."

"I'm not going to fool around."

"Sure. Don't call the police, don't do anything except sit in that chair until either I show up or I call to tell you there was nothing I could do and your kid is dead."

"Hey—"

"You never know which way the wind will blow, Roger."

Stiletto opened the office door and slipped into the hallway. He hurried back to his rental and started the motor. The clock was ticking. He had to work fast.

The night was still warm, and Stiletto felt sweat trickling down his back as he hustled up the road leading to the cabin Damien had secured near the Snake River. He couldn't see it, but he heard the rippling water as it flowed. The sound wasn't enough to cover his footsteps, so he stayed focused on moving a little, stopping, then moving forward some more until he reached the border of the property and the trees marking the boundary.

Stiletto was ready for action. Colt .45 under his left arm, Kriss Vector secured on a sling, spare magazines for each weapon standing by. Wire garrote in the right pocket of his coat. The Ka-Bar knife rode on his right hip. Hooked to his belt on the left were the two flash-bangs. The night was going to get much hotter than the posted temperature very soon.

The moon gave him enough light to get a sense of the movements around him. He was looking for the four out-of-town gunmen Damien had hired who were undoubtedly being used to guard Peter Ivy. Stiletto spotted Damien's Challenger near the front of the house but saw no sign of the truck used in the kidnapping. They'd probably ditched it on the way or were in the process of getting rid of the vehicle.

Stiletto examined the windows along the side of the house. Only one showed any light within. The other two remained dark.

Stiletto listened as the crickets, which had gone silent upon his arrival, resumed chirping. Any trooper worth his salt would listen for a change in the crickets' chirping, and when Scott spotted a lone sentry coming around the back of the house, he knew somebody had indeed noticed and was on the way to take a look.

Where were the other three? Inside? What about Damien and his crew? The raid would be for naught if Stiletto couldn't nail the wild bunch in one place. The last thing he wanted was for them to scatter in different directions. It would leave only the old man for him to deal with, and that wouldn't avenge Shelly Pierce's murder. The real killer would be in the wind.

It had to end here. Tonight. Shelly Pierce and Chad Mendoza, not to mention countless others Stiletto wasn't aware of, deserved revenge, and they would have it tonight.

Stiletto stayed on his belly and watched the trooper get closer. He held no weapon; his hands were free. That meant the hardware was under his coat. He probably didn't like the heat of the night any more than Stiletto. The shooter stopped in the middle of the yard and looked around. The crickets had resumed, so perhaps he wasn't going to conduct a full circuit.

Which put him out of range for a close-up kill using the garrotes.

No matter.

Stiletto flicked off the safety on the Kriss Vector. The short barrel was extended a few inches by a thick sound suppressor. Stiletto kept the folded shoulder stock closed and peered through the infrared Aimpoint sight atop the weapon.

He placed the red dot on the man's chest and fired one round. The Kriss Vector spat, the snap-click of the action the only sound as the .45 hollow-point exited the suppressor tube and flashed toward its target. Stiletto kept the gunman centered in the Aimpoint. The slug smacked the target where Stiletto intended, a subtle movement of the man's shirt indicating impact. The shooter dropped, and Stiletto didn't waste time. He broke cover and, staying low, moved toward the fallen man. He flicked the selector switch on the Vector to full-auto in case of a surprise.

He found no radio on the man, but a compact Heckler & Koch MP5-K was holstered under his coat. Stiletto left the 9mm machine pistol and began a slow crawl to the side of the house. He wanted to see into one of the windows.

He reached the wall close to the rear, where more open grass awaited. He couldn't see around the corner to scan the back porch but figured that was where the shooter he'd taken out had come from. Moving along the wall, Scott stopped at the first darkened window and slowly raised his head to look over the sill. There was enough light from down a connecting hallway that Stiletto recognized a kitchen counter and corner table.

Dropping back, he reversed his crawl and looked around the back corner. The back porch was a small deck with steps and a sitting area. The awning covering the rear door. Stiletto probed beneath the deck; nobody hiding there. He started up the wooden steps with the Vector out and ready. The wood under his feet creaked a little.

He paused as the outline of a man appeared in the window of the back door. The door swung open, the man leaning out to say something, but whatever was on his mind died with him as the Vector whispered a stream of slugs that ripped the gunman from abdomen to chest.

Scott dodged out of the way as the gunner's body tumbled down the steps, the HK under his coat falling from its holster as he settled on the ground.

There was shouting from inside. Stiletto tugged a flash-bang from his belt, let the Vector dangle on its sling, and pulled the pin. He pitched the grenade through the door and dropped to one knee, turning his head away and shutting his eyes as the flash-bang detonated within.

The back of the house lit up brightly as the concussion blast echoed through the night. Stiletto gripped the Vector in both hands as he raced through the doorway, bent over. He swung the muzzle left and right, but he had no targets. Pushing forward, he stopped short as he found an older man on his knees, both hands over his ears, his eyes shut tight. Scott stitched him with a burst of rounds, stepped over his fallen body, and continued into a hallway. He nearly collided with the fourth hired gunman, both men reacting quickly, the goon raising one arm to block Stiletto's advance and the other fist for a quick right cross.

Stiletto lifted a foot into the man's groin. The gunman let out a yell and bent over, Scott stepping aside and raising a knee into the man's face. Bone crunched. The gunner landed hard, and Stiletto blasted him in the back of the head.

Stiletto dropped the empty magazine and slapped a new one into the Vector's receiver as his eyes scanned for more targets and his ears picked up various sounds.

More shouting. Panicked shouting, too, from people

who weren't used to being under attack with military weapons. Stiletto smiled. The wild bunch was about to meet its match.

He heard another kind of panicked yelling from elsewhere in the house too.

Somebody shouting, "Let me out of here! Let me out!"

When Peter Ivy finally woke up, he wasn't in his car.

He was on his side on a cold floor, surrounded by bars. As his vision cleared, he realized he was in a cage. He tried to stand up but bumped his head. He had to hunch over. He rattled the bars. He was locked solidly inside.

He shouted. Loudly. For a long time. He stopped shouting when Damien Swanberg entered the room holding a revolver.

"Shut up or I'll kill you."

"What's going on, Damien? The hell are you doing?"

"You're going to stay put until your father comes across with his cartel connection, and then maybe we'll let you go."

Peter Ivy let out a string of curses at Swanberg the Younger, but Damien only laughed as he turned and left the room.

Now there were explosions going off in the house, and men screaming, crashing, and thudding. Peter Ivy shook the door of the cage some more, yelling, "Let me out of here! Let me out!"

Nobody answered.

Instead, gunshots popped. Peter Ivy jumped with each shot, suddenly wishing his cage had more room in which to hide.

Damien Swanberg's pulse raced as the flash-bang popped, the bright light flaring for a moment before blinking out.

Damien, Joe Armstrong, Teddy Stone, and Eric Foster turned over furniture in the living room and hid behind the couches and love seat. The TV was now off, their formerly carefree period of waiting for Roger Ivy's call about the cartel connection long forgotten as they faced the possibility of armed gunmen.

Damien kept checking behind him. There was a window there, but nobody came through.

"How many are there?" Eric said, his voice shaking.

"Shut up!" Damien shouted.

"Where are the guys we hired?" Joe yelled. He kept transferring his revolver to his left hand, so he could wipe his sweaty right hand on his jeans.

"Shut up!" Damien repeated.

He swallowed hard and wished he had a bigger weapon than the snub-nosed .38 Special. The only "combat training" he and his pals had experienced came from Saturday afternoon paintball outings where you might get your clothes splattered with multi-colored paint, but nobody died.

In the real gunfight they were facing, they all might die.

Was this Roger Ivy's doing? Were his cartel buddies stepping into the game?

The dark hallway might as well have been a black hole as Damien waited for whoever was down there to show himself. Part of him sensed he was being drawn into the hole, where he'd meet only his doom.

Stiletto stayed low and close to the wall and stared down the hallway to the end. He'd heard the furniture tumbling over and the panicked conversation, so he knew where his quarry was. But they had to have access to an exit. A patio door, something. He had to hurry.

He tugged his last flash-bang from his belt, pulled the pin, and rolled the grenade down the hall. It curved toward the wall, bouncing off, and entering the living room at an angle. Stiletto covered his eyes as the blast and flash of light filled the hallway. As soon as it faded, he charged down the hall with the Kriss Vector up and ready.

The wild bunch was scattered around, moaning and wailing from the grenade's concussive blast, and Stiletto picked out his first target.

Joe Armstrong.

The gang's driver was behind a loveseat, partially exposed, his gun forgotten on the floor as he clamped a hand over his eyes to relieve the pain from the flash. Stiletto shot him through the side of the head. His body jerked once and lay still.

Stiletto pivoted, the muzzle passing over the larger couch and continuing to the other side of the room, where Teddy Stone and the fourth gang member, Eric Foster, tried to regain cover and raise their weapons. Stiletto stroked the Vector's trigger. His first burst pinned Eric Foster to the wall, punching multiple fist-sized holes through his body that no amount of time in the hospital would fix.

Teddy Stone managed to raise his gun but not before Stiletto's next burst punched through his neck and jaw, taking most of the bottom of his face away as the force of impact flung his body to the ground.

The couch!

Stiletto pivoted again as Damien Swanberg launched himself over the overturned couch, the .38 extended. Stiletto dove as Swanberg fired three rapid rounds and rolled out of the way as Damien hit the floor. Scott scrambled to his feet at the same time as Damien, both rising, Stiletto firing at where the younger Swanberg had been. His burst tore up the carpet, the Vector's bolt locking back over the empty magazine.

Damien didn't stick around but charged into the next room. Stiletto letting the Vector fall at his side while he snatched the Colt .45 from leather and charged after him. Scott banged his shoulder going through the doorway as Damien ran to the front of the house, crashing through the front door. Stiletto braced in the doorway and fired once but missed. He ran after Damien, who apparently had forgotten the .38 in his hand because he didn't try to shoot back as he ran to his car.

Stiletto fired again. His shot kicked up the grass at Damien's feet, the bullet nicking the heel of his left shoe. Damien stumbled mid-stride, falling forward and crashing hard into the driver's side of the Challenger, landing in a heap.

Stiletto held the .45 casually in his right hand and walked the distance to the fallen young man.

Damien struggled to get up, the .38 forgotten as he pawed for his car keys, snapping a frightened glance over his shoulder at the oncoming big man who'd wiped out his crew.

"Stop! Stay away!"

Stiletto laughed.

Damien remembered the .38 and, taking his eyes off Stiletto, reached for the gun. He swung up his arm, but when he fired, Stiletto wasn't there.

Scott had run to the rear of the Challenger while Damien wasn't looking, trading the .45 for one of the wire garrotes. He now leaned over Swanberg the Younger, the garrote pulled taut as he wrapped the wire around the man's neck. Scott yanked as hard as he could, almost dragging Damien with him as he crossed one fist over the other and let the wire cut into his flesh.

Damien yelled, his hands flashing to his neck, then to Stiletto's hands, banging against Scott's balled fists in vain.

A trickle of blood from Damien's sliced skin flowed

from the slice onto the garrote wire and down his shirt.

Damien's struggles continued. He dug his feet into the ground to try to push back against Stiletto's firmly-planted body, Scott turning with Damien's twists and keeping the pressure on his neck.

Stiletto ignored the sweat coating his face as he held steady, a picture of Shelly Pierce firmly in his mind's eye and the words in her diary front and center in his thoughts as Damien Swanberg struggled for his last breath. He'd taken everything she'd had, every hope, every dream. He'd snuffed out her and Chad Mendoza like a normal person swatting a fly. His father, an even worse specimen, had encouraged the effort.

Their reign of terror ended tonight!

Scott did not let up. He pulled harder, straining his arms. A drop of sweat fell off the tip of his nose onto his lower lip. The salty taste brought Stiletto back to reality.

Damien's choked cries, loud at first, began to soften. Damien's struggles, violent at the start, began to weaken. When his hands finally fell limply to each side, Stiletto let go.

Damien's body dropped solidly beside his car, the wire embedded in his neck slickly red.

Damien Swanberg had had a lot to answer for, and Stiletto had sent him to his Maker to answer those questions before he arrived at his ultimate destination.

That was above Scott's pay grade.

Stiletto felt in Damien's pocket for the keys to the

Challenger. He found Damien's cell phone a few feet away and checked to make sure the phone wasn't locked by a code or thumbprint. It wasn't. Damien had left the phone wide open.

He used the key-fob remote to open the trunk of the car and loaded Damien's body inside.

Then he returned to the house to retrieve Peter Ivy.

The night was still young, and there was much left to accomplish.

CHAPTER FORTY-SEVEN

Stiletto collected a stunned but compliant Peter Ivy from the cage, escorting him past the bloating bodies to the Challenger, where Damien lay. Peter did not offer any reaction to the sight of the body. Stiletto helped him into the passenger side of the car, took his position behind the wheel, and powered out of there.

Presently, Peter Ivy asked, "Where are you taking me?"

"Back to your father."

"Okay."

"I don't hear you asking why this happened," Stiletto said.

Peter Ivy scoffed. "I know why. I'm not an idiot. Neither are you."

"You sure thought I was one the other night."

"Sorry about that."

Now Stiletto scoffed, shaking his head. "You told me too much anyway. The path I started on that night led me straight to this house."

Peter Ivy sank in the seat a little.

Stiletto drove back toward the city. The next phase of the plan was taking shape in his mind, and now he was glad that Vince Six had provided his cell number.

Stiletto would require the enforcer's assistance during the next phase, and planned to obtain that assistance with an offer the Mafioso couldn't refuse.

Stiletto laughed. Peter Ivy didn't ask him what was so funny.

He held Six's business card and the steering wheel with one hand, dialing with the other. He hoped the enforcer would answer the line despite not knowing the number.

"Who is this?" Six asked after two rings.

"Stiletto. I have Damien Swanberg's body in the trunk."

Peter Ivy's eyes widened. Stiletto winked at him.

"You work fast."

"I'm going to call his father and tell him to come and get the body, but I need a location."

"There's a warehouse you can use, hang on." Six went away for a moment. "Got a pen?"

"I'm driving. Tell me how to get there."

Six relayed the directions. Stiletto asked him to repeat one or two parts.

"You didn't only call me to tell me you had a body in the trunk."

"Once Swanberg leaves his place," Stiletto said, "you might want to have some guys go in there and take advantage of whatever information your insiders gave you."

"I'm picking up what you're putting down."

"Don't tell Chloe."

"My lips are sealed."

Stiletto ended the call and dropped the phone into the cupholder in the center console.

Peter Ivy said, "There's really a dead body in the trunk?"

"Relax," Stiletto said. "It's not yours."

Peter Ivy let out a groan and leaned against the car door.

The Challenger's tires screeched as Stiletto abruptly stopped, not caring that he'd parked crooked across two spaces. He helped Peter Ivy out of the car, and once the younger man stood to full height, he seemed to recover whatever strength he'd lost between the house and the club. Maybe being so close to his father once again after a harrowing night was refueling his gas tank.

Stiletto grabbed his upper left arm anyway, hauled him quickly into the club, and shoved him through the doorway of his father's office.

Peter cursed as he stumbled, quickly landing in a chair and glaring at Scott.

Roger Ivy jumped around his desk and grabbed his son, hugging him tightly. Stiletto used both hands to pull the two men apart.

"Later," he said. "You got something for me, Roger?"

"Yeah, yeah," Roger Ivy grabbed a tote bag from his desk. He unzipped it to show Stiletto the laptop inside, a compact Dell that looked well-used. "Everything is there. Contacts, proposed routes—everything you need."

Stiletto stared at the man.

"I'm not lying, I swear. On the life of my kid, this is everything you need."

Stiletto took the tote and closed the zipper sharply. Roger Ivy recoiled a little. "You better get out of town," Stiletto said. "Once I'm done with the cartel, anybody left alive is going to know who sold them out."

Stiletto glanced at Peter, then back at Roger. Peter was shaking a little. Roger seemed small.

"Behave yourselves," said.

Then he turned and went out. He climbed back into the Challenger. As he cycled through Damien's cell phone for his father's number, he thought about what he'd said to Six.

Don't tell Chloe.

He had the collection of files Boskowictz had provided, and he was going to give that information to Giordana.

He didn't know why.

Or maybe he did. As he pressed Send to call Swanberg, he knew exactly why he wasn't taking down the Giordana syndicate along with Swanberg, the puppet master.

He couldn't bring himself to separate a father from his daughter.

Chloe and Ben Giordana were far apart already. A prison sentence or worse might mean they never reconciled.

And Stiletto held out hope that they would.

Because he also hoped he might reconcile with Felicia someday.

Ben Giordana and his Outfit syndicate had caused their share of grief, committed an unknown number of crimes, and needed to be put down like the rabid dogs they were. But dammit, even gangsters loved their kids, and Stiletto placated his contrary thoughts with the reasoning that nothing they had done had crossed his radar. Swanberg, on the other hand, deserved his wrath, and more.

Stiletto stopped thinking. He was twisting his brain into a pretzel trying to figure out why he was going to let Giordana off the hook. Leave Twin Falls in the same bad shape as he'd found it, basically. He found his earlier resolve to tear the place apart fading, the more he thought about the woman at the diner and the man in the penthouse.

The call rang, then somebody picked up.

"It's late, Damien. There better not be a problem."

"Sorry, Pops," Stiletto greeted him.

"Who is this?"

"You might know me as 'the mystery man.' The one you tried to kill. The one your men missed. Remember?"

"Why are you calling me on my son's phone?"

"Grim tone. I like that, Kurt. You know something is wrong, but you can't quite bring yourself to admit what you feel in your gut."

"Are you going to answer me?"

"Your son's body is in the trunk of his car, and I'm behind the wheel. I'd like you to come and collect the body before it stinks up the place."

Silence.

"Damien is dead, Kurt. I almost sliced off his head using a garrote."

Swanberg said nothing. Scott listened to him breathe heavily for a moment, then resumed talking. He told Swanberg the address of the warehouse and said he'd be there alone, waiting with dear, departed Damien. They had business to settle, and Stiletto added that he didn't intend for that business to take longer than a few minutes.

"And if you don't believe me," Stiletto added, "check out the house where your son and his gang were holding Peter Ivy. I guarantee you everybody else had a quicker exit than your kid."

Swanberg finally mustered a response.

"You're a dead man."

Stiletto laughed and ended the call with a swipe of his thumb.

CHAPTER FORTY-EIGHT

Carl Boskowictz packed his life into two suitcases.

He wasn't much of a clotheshorse, so he planned to take care of his wardrobe at his new location, wherever that turned out to be. Right now, all he wanted to do was get out of Twin Falls.

The other case contained whatever personal items he decided he couldn't live without, mostly books and knick-knacks. Items that were certainly replaceable, but gave his place the color it lacked when only he occupied it. The only non-replaceable items in the second case were the framed photos of his late wife.

He zipped the second case closed and wandered around the apartment, looking at what he planned to leave behind. Nothing struck him as a must-have on this pass. The apartment manager could set everything on fire for all he cared.

There was a knock on the door.

Boskowictz took a deep breath. He didn't approach the

door but instead called out from a few feet away.

"Who's there?"

"It's Vince."

"It's too late for a visit."

"I need your help, Carl."

Boskowictz stared at the door. He shook his head and answered, "I'm leaving town, Vince."

"Can I come in?"

"No."

"He did it."

"Who did what?"

"Stiletto. Chloe's friend. He whacked Swanberg's kid, and now he's going to have the old man collect the body."

Boskowictz whistled, despite the interruption in his travel plans. "That's impressive."

Six told him where the meeting was going to take place. "He's alone. Swanberg will bring a crew. I know you're packed, but how about one last time? Let's go cover the guy's backside."

Boskowictz blinked.

"What's on your mind?" Six asked.

"Nothing. I only want to get out of here."

"Help me with this, and you're a free man."

"Really?"

"As free as you allow yourself to be, Carl."

"I didn't know you were a philosopher."

"Can we talk about this in the car?"

"Yeah. Let me get my gun."

Stiletto followed Addison Avenue East until he arrived at the darkened warehouse Vince Six had described. The structure was well separated from neighbors, generic enough for the average person never to notice it was there, and surrounded by a fence. Six had described the fence, adding that the gate wasn't locked when the warehouse wasn't being used, as was the case currently. Stiletto hadn't asked what the warehouse was used for. Six had provided the door code for the rear entrance, and that was where Stiletto steered the Challenger.

Leaving the car running, he climbed out and examined the exit. The electronic keypad responded to his input and the lock snapped back. He went inside the darkened warehouse and felt for a light switch, finding it off to the left. A section of lights snapped on, but most of the building remained dark. Stiletto hunted for a way to open the rear doors, finally locating the opening mechanism and pressing the button. With a rumble, the rear door rolled upward. Stiletto pressed the button again to stop it once he had enough room to bring the Challenger inside. He parked diagonally, the passenger door facing the opening. Then he climbed out again, lit a cigar, and used his cell phone flashlight to explore the rest of the facility.

As he'd thought, it was wide open, with offices off to

one side and some clutter and dust on the floor. In the right corner, several stacks of pallets maybe six feet high sat quietly. There were probably spiders hiding in the pallets, but the stacks made for good cover. A stray forklift caught his attention, as well.

He dropped to one knee behind it.

The Colt Combat Government, reloaded, hung under his left arm as usual, and he had easy access to the Kriss Vector, minus the suppressor. The stubby submachine gun rode on its sling under his right arm. All set for Swanberg and whatever party he wanted to bring.

He puffed on his H. Upmann and looked around some more. No second floor. No rafters for a sniper to hide in. The building existed solely as a temporary storage area, and Stiletto again forced his thoughts away from what the Outfit might store here. He was sure a great deal of stolen property, stolen cars, illegal weapons, and drug shipments had occupied the space at one time or another.

Could he really turn over Boskowictz's insurance file to Giordana, the man who least deserved the material?

What other options did he have?

A car rumbled outside.

Stiletto watched the partially open door. He had the Challenger's key fob in hand. One press of the button and the trunk lid would pop. Swanberg could lift the lid and look at his kid lying dead in the trunk, which would be the last thing his eyes saw. That was when Stiletto intended to put a bullet through his head.

Headlights flashed through the gap in the rear door, and the car stopped halfway in. The passenger door flew open and a big man in a white suit stomped into the warehouse, a grim set to his face but no weapon in his hand. The other four who exited the car, including the driver, carried the hardware. Heckler & Koch 416 carbines. They weren't messing around. The HKs were military-grade and fired the potent 5.56mm NATO round.

"Guess I'm outgunned," Stiletto called.

Swanberg and his gun crew looked around but couldn't pinpoint his spot.

Swanberg shouted, "Where's my son? Where?"

Swanberg approached the trunk as he moved around the car. Scott pressed the trunk button on the key fob.

The lid popped open.

"Have a look," Stiletto yelled.

The shooters moved around to the driver's side of the car, blocking most of Scott's view of Swanberg, but he saw enough.

As Swanberg lifted the trunk lid, the hinges squeaked. He stared inside for a moment, the color draining from his face as he took in the sight of his son, and then he let out an anguished cry.

Stiletto took out the Kriss Vector submachine gun and clicked off the safety.

CHAPTER FORTY-NINE

"Kill him! Kill him now!"

Stiletto lifted the Vector to his shoulder. He had the momentary advantage of the gunmen being in the light, but he'd lose that advantage after the first burst. Such is life.

The Vector spat, the buzz-saw-like sound of the firing echoing in the warehouse. One of the gunners fell, his face twisted in pain as the .45 slugs cut through him. His weapon scraped across the cement floor.

The other two raised their weapons, shouting for Swanberg to get to cover, but the man in white didn't leave the trunk. His focus remained on his son's body. The HKs fired, Stiletto pressing to the cold floor as the 5.56mm slugs whined around him, tearing through the wall behind him and rocking the forklift. The vinyl seat exploded with bullet strikes, stuffing flying from the cushion and seatback. Stiletto scooted around the front of the vehicle and let another burst go.

His salvo didn't strike any targets, but the gunners scattered, one grabbing Swanberg and forcing him to the passenger side of the car. They were exposed for a moment, and Stiletto took the shot. He didn't aim for Swanberg. His burst stitched a line across the back of the shooter, punching through his neck and splattering Swanberg with gore as he collapsed. Some sense finally entered Swanberg's brains and he took cover, but then rose over the roof with the HK carbine in both hands. Yelling, he sprayed a long burst.

The rounds danced around Scott's position, popping one of the tires. The forklift sank as the air left the tire, and Scott hurriedly scooted for the pallets, firing a covering burst to keep Swanberg and the remaining pair of gunners pinned down.

Swanberg shouted again, "Kill him! I want his body!"

Stiletto watched the gunners through a gap in the pallets. He yelled, "Tina Lawson sends her regards!"

"Kill him now!"

The two remaining shooters took his positions at the front and rear bumper. They fired short bursts, still aiming for the forklift. From his spot behind the pallets, Stiletto didn't have a good angle to fire on either. He needed to move, but there was nowhere else to go. My kingdom for a hand grenade.

Lights flashed on throughout the warehouse, Stiletto shutting his eyes against the sudden glare. When he opened them, he saw how precarious his position actually was. The stack of pallets only partially covered him, the next stack too far away to cover the part of him that was exposed. The shooter immediately spotted him through the gap.

They turned the HK carbines on him faster than he could get the Vector to his shoulder. Stiletto dropped and rolled as the salvos shattered the pallets, wood chips flying in all direction. Scott rolled into the open, staying flat as he returned fire, the Vector ejecting spent rounds that clinked onto the floor. He tagged one of the shooters, the gunman at the rear bumper, who let out a yell as he tipped over. The Vector clicked empty. Scott jumped up and ran to his right. Across the floor were the offices and another place to hide, but they also represented a kill box. There was only one way in or out, and if the remaining shooter, and Swanberg, deployed tactics properly, they might easily trap him within.

A burst of rounds smacked into the floor, a slug nicking Stiletto's left leg as it ricocheted, and Stiletto plunged headlong to the ground. He landed on his chest, the wind rushing out of him, his grip on the Vector lost. The submachine gun spun away and hit the wall ahead.

Stiletto rolled onto his back and snatched the Colt .45 from the shoulder holster. He brought up the pistol in both hands. The last shooter had left his position to close in for a kill shot and Scott caught him in the open, lining him up in the Colt's night sights and easing back the trigger. The

.45 spoke once. The gunner stopped as if he'd hit a wall and fell over.

Scott breathed hard as he kept the pistol trained on the car, waiting for Swanberg to break cover. He had plenty of hardware to access if he was brave enough to risk exposure.

Then a grin pulled at Stiletto's mouth.

Swanberg didn't know how to hide behind a car, and his feet were partially visible under it. It was a tricky shot, but Stiletto took up the slack on the trigger and let a round go. He missed, the round sparking off the concrete under the Challenger, but came close enough that Swanberg let out a yell and jumped up to run outside.

The move exposed his back. Stiletto fired again, the .45's action snapping back and ejecting the spent round, which struck the floor near Stiletto at the same moment the slug ripped into Swanberg's crisp white suit.

Kurt Swanberg's arms flew up as he fell forward. Stiletto jumped to his feet and limped across the warehouse floor, moving around the pooling blood from the gunmen. Swanberg struggled to rise, the .45 having ripped open his left shoulder, red soaking into the white suit.

Scott kicked Swanberg in the side, causing him to cry out, and turned him over on his back. Swanberg, gasping, stared up him.

Stiletto squatted beside the man.

"Sucks, don't it?" he said.

"You—"

Stiletto's left hand moved in a flash. He backhanded Swanberg across the face.

"Tina Lawson. Shelly Pierce. Chad Mendoza. Erin Keene. Do those names mean anything to you?"

Swanberg groaned, his face strained. "You'll never leave this city alive," he said.

"One of us won't."

Stiletto stood and casually fired a slug into Swanberg's head. Blood spattered on Scott's shoes, and he wiped them on the white suit.

Headlights flashed across Stiletto as another car pulled behind the warehouse.

CHAPTER FIFTY

Scott brought up the .45, moving back to the cover of the warehouse. He slipped under the door and hustled despite his limp for one of the dead gunners, snatching up an HK. He held the weapon ready as he squatted beside the car.

"Stiletto!"

Scott let out a breath and tossed the weapon aside. He recognized the voice of Vince Six.

Outside, he met Six and Carl Boskowictz, both carrying their handguns, both curiously looking at the carnage.

"You're late," Stiletto said. "But thanks for coming."

"You obviously didn't need any help." Six holstered his SIG-Sauer, and Boskowictz put away his revolver.

The three men stood over the body of Kurt Swanberg, silently regarding the dead man, the man of power, who lived no more.

"Did you send guys to his place?" Stiletto asked.

"Large crew, like you suggested," Six said. "They had a nice fight with Swanberg's remaining guys, but they're tearing the place apart. They've already cleared the safe."

Stiletto said nothing, He kept his attention on the body and didn't acknowledge that Six was looking at him.

"What are your plans now?" Six said.

Stiletto shook his head. "I did what I came to do. Ben Giordana was a pawn in a bigger game, controlled by this piece of garbage, so I don't have a beef with him."

"Good, because we'd leave you here if you did," Six said.

Stiletto grinned at Six.

"Do you really think so?"

Six laughed. "We'd try really hard, at least."

Stiletto and Six laughed. Boskowictz remained stoic. Six turned to the police sergeant.

"Something on your mind, Carl?"

"I'm done here," Boskowictz said.

"I know you are. I'll take you back to your apartment, and you can carry on."

Boskowictz nodded.

"Sergeant," Stiletto said.

Boskowictz turned to Scott.

"Whatever you do next," Stiletto said, "do it right."

"I will," he said, adding, "But as the only officially empowered police officer at this location, I suggest we clear out."

"It's a Giordana property," Six said. "We have plenty of time."

"For what?" Stiletto asked.

"To call another crew and make these bodies disap-pear."

The Boskowictz File, the police sergeant's "insurance policy," which he had gifted to Stiletto, mocked Scott as it sat on the table in his hotel room. He stared at the file from the edge of the bed.

The sun would be up in a few hours, the daylight still unable to penetrate the drapes across the windows.

There was no way, after all, that he could hand the file over to Giordana. Whether to let the Outfit's boss remain in power wasn't his decision to make, but his day of reckoning was due; of that, Stiletto had no doubt. There was one other person he could deliver the information to. He'd trust her to do the right thing when she was ready. When she was, perhaps then Twin Falls could emerge from the boot under which it was living.

Stiletto undressed and took a long shower, then stretched out on the bed, but didn't try to sleep. He laid there looking at the ceiling, and when the clock finally showed seven a.m., he dressed again and went out with the Boskowictz File tucked under his arm.

A waitress at Chloe's Diner sat him in his preferred back-corner booth, and Scott ordered breakfast and asked to see Chloe if she was around. The waitress promised to get her, but returned a few moments later and said the boss was not available.

Stiletto ate his breakfast and drank his tea quietly as the morning rush carried on around him. Was she still upset about their meeting with her father, or was she refusing to see him because she now equated him with her father and wasn't going to say a word to him?

Stiletto paid his check and tipped his waitress and then asked if he could go back and see Chloe. The waitress pointed the way. Stiletto went around the counter and down a short hallway packed on either side with boxes and found Chloe's office. The door was shut. He turned the knob and entered.

Chloe, behind her desk, snapped up her head. "I said—" She stopped.

"It's me."

"Get out."

Stiletto shut the door. He held the bundle in front of him.

"I said, get out."

"Chloe—"

"No. I want nothing more to do with you, Scott. Leave."

"Chloe, please."

"Are you deaf? All that gunfire ruin your hearing?"

Stiletto let out a breath but didn't take his eyes off the woman behind the desk. Her eyes were hot, her mouth a straight line. Her blonde hair was pulled back in a tight bun, no rebellious strands breaking free. She sat straight up in her chair, the paperwork on the desk forgotten, the pen she held still firmly gripped in her right hand.

"I did what I came to do."

"I heard."

"What do you mean?"

"Six called me late last night and told me."

"I see."

"If you're done, why are you still here?"

"I wanted to say good-bye."

"Good-bye. Now go."

"Chloe."

She threw down the pen. "What?"

Stiletto set the Boskowictz file on her already-cluttered desk and explained what was inside.

"What am I supposed to do with this?" she asked.

"Whatever you want."

"What I want is to be left alone to live my life without a bunch of killers getting in my way."

"And your daughter."

"What about her?"

"You want her back too, right?"

"Of course."

"It's up to you what to do with that information. If you hand it over to federal law enforcement, you can change this city for the better."

"As opposed to how you didn't change it?"

"I had my reasons."

"Which were?"

"My daughter isn't talking to me, Chloe, probably for the same reasons you aren't talking to your father. I'd like to think she and I can connect again someday. I hope you and your father can, too."

"So you've left his syndicate fully intact, with all of its associated corruption and crime, because you have a soft spot?"

"It's what makes me different from all those other killers, Chloe. You think about that."

"I'll be thinking about no such thing, thank you very much."

Stiletto opened his mouth to say something more, but Chloe's anger was undeniable.

"Good-bye, Chloe," he said. He opened the door and stepped out.

She didn't respond to his farewell.

CHAPTER FIFTY-ONE

Stiletto waited at the Greyhound station for the next bus out of Twin Falls, Idaho. He wasn't sure where he was going. He'd bought a ticket for the West Coast simply to get on the road. Once he settled somewhere, however temporary the stop, he'd contact The Trust and re-open the conversation about joining the organization full-time and finding a way to remove the Russian gunsights from his back.

He sat on the hard bench with his luggage at his feet and activity all him around that he paid no attention to. He knew he should be paying attention. That somewhere nearby, a threat might exist, but his mind was too numb to process details.

Chloe had been right. He was leaving Twin Falls basically as he found it, with Ben Giordana probably even more empowered now that the specter of Kurt Swanberg no longer existed.

He'd come to Twin Falls to deliver a message. He'd found the intended recipient, Shelly Pierce, dead. Murdered. He'd set out to solve the crime and avenge her death, but in the process, he'd disturbed a much larger ecosystem with a stranglehold on the city. He had wanted to explain to Chloe that while he usually conducted himself in a cold and calculated manner, the situation in Twin Falls had made such dispassion impossible to maintain. He'd always blended compassion with action, but this time, the former overruled the latter. He might have been a killer, as Chloe said, but he wasn't a programmed machine incapable of making his own choices, choices he made because a father and daughter were in conflict with one another, and the daughter was unwilling to negotiate peace.

Would it have been worth the cost to remove Giordana as well? Would Chloe still have been angry after the dust settled? Might she have been worse off had he left her world in pieces and moved on to the next fight?

Was he doing any good at all?

Stiletto looked up as the hydraulic brakes of his bus hissed. The bus pulled up to the curb, and passengers began lining up to board. Stiletto stepped into line with them and boarded the bus with a bitter-sour taste on his tongue—the taste of defeat. After he settled into his seat, he stared out the window at nothing in particular, and only felt a sense of relief when the bus pulled onto the interstate.

He was leaving Twin Falls and a lot of pain, uncertainty, and doubt behind, and going forward into an unknown future with no easy answers.

Vince "Six" Coburn stepped out of the penthouse elevator and nodded hello to the guards at the main door. He went into penthouse but didn't see Giordana on the balcony.

"In here, Vince."

Six walked into Giordana's study. Unlike most people, Giordana didn't favor full bookshelves, but instead had hung abstract paintings that filled only some of the white space on the walls. The boss of the Twin Falls syndicate sat behind a kidney-shaped desk. He gestured to the chair in front of the desk, and Six dutifully sat.

Giordana reclined his seat a little. "All cleaned up?"

"Squeaky," Six said.

"Swanberg's place?"

"We should have any material pertinent to us within an hour."

"You watch those guys, Six. If anybody tries to hold anything back to use against me, I want them dealt with."

"Yes, sir."

"We're going to have a meeting with the boys tomorrow or the next day," Giordana said. "Everything is like it was, and more so. I want the word to go out to any

Swanberg stragglers, especially Doug Armstrong and his bunch, that they're either with us or they'll be put in the ground. Clear?"

"Crystal."

Six suppressed a smile because Giordana would want to know what was so funny.

The Outfit boss was dressed smartly, as usual, and his hair was cut close to his scalp. He was energized and ready for action.

"If Roger Ivy and his family aren't out of town by the end of the day, set the club on fire. When he and his family are gone, set the club on fire. I want that place torched."

"Yes, sir."

"Where's Boskowictz?"

"On the road."

"Tell you where?" Giordana said.

"No."

"He leave anything behind?"

"Most of his possessions are still in his apartment," Six said. "I don't think he left behind anything to incriminate us if that's what you're afraid of. He only wanted out of here."

"All right."

Giordana rocked in his chair.

"What else is on your mind, Ben?"

"Next Monday, I want you back on my granddaughter's trail."

"Okay."

Giordana's bluster faded and his shoulders sank a little. "Maybe my daughter will come around if you can bring Monica home."

"I'll do my best, Ben. I almost found her last time."

"I hope you can pick up the trail again."

"No sweat."

"Okay, Six. Thanks. That's all."

Vince Six left the chair and exited the office. He nodded good-bye to the guards and entered the elevator for the ride down.

Business as usual. Back to basics. No more Swanberg.

Six had no doubt in his mind that they had dodged a bullet with Mr. Scott Stiletto. He could have easily burned the syndicate to the ground.

When the elevator let him off on the ground floor, Six wondered why he hadn't. He thought he knew the answer, but he didn't quite believe it. Evidence suggested, though, that he wasn't wrong. Stiletto had pulled back because of Chloe, and probably only she knew why. For Six, the truth would almost certainly remain a mystery.

He'd never forget the mystery man, though, and hoped they never crossed paths again.

Chloe Giordana sat behind her desk and cried.

The bundle Stiletto had left remained on her desk, and after wiping her eyes, she transported it to a shelf behind her, where she dropped it with other forgotten items to be attended to later.

How dare he drop that in her lap?

But what had she truly expected of him? He was a human being, not a Wild West gunfighter riding into Twin Falls on a horse to dispatch evil villains and free the town.

Did she have the right to be angry at him?

She didn't want to think about what he had said about her and her father. As far as Chloe was concerned, her father could die alone in his penthouse, making excuses for why nothing he'd ever done was truly his fault.

She sniffed. She would continue managing her own life without interference. She'd faced her share of difficulties and tragedies and had always carried through. If nothing else, her father had instilled within her persistence in the face of any obstacle. She was grateful for that, even though she hated his guts.

The phone on her desk rang, the jangle breaking her reverie and filling the office with noise after a long silence.

She ignored the phone. It rang again.

With a grunt, she lifted the receiver.

"Hello?"

No response. The line was open—she heard the telltale buzz—but nobody spoke on the other end.

"Is anybody there?" Chloe said.

Finally, a woman's voice crackled over the line.

"Mom?"

IF YOU LIKED THIS BOOK, CHECK OUT THE DANGEROUS MR. WOLF

MR. WOLF IS A BRAND-NEW HERO THAT YOU CAN ROOT FOR FROM THE AUTHOR OF THE HARD-EDGED SCOTT STILETTO THRILLERS – BRIAN DRAKE.

When innocent people are in the crossfire and the police are unable to help, Wolf picks up where the law leaves off.

As he hunts for clues through the city's dark alleys, chasing mafia killers, solving a decades-old crime, or helping a widow unravel the mystery behind a murder attempt, he quickly uncovers the hidden hands behind the violence, but even he isn't ready for the shocking twists when the last bullets are fired.

THE DANGEROUS MR. WOLF is your introduction to a good man to have on your side.

Better pray he stays there.

AVAILABLE NOW ON AMAZON

ABOUT THE AUTHOR

A twenty-five year veteran of radio and television broadcasting, Brian Drake has spent his career in San Francisco where he's filled writing, producing, and reporting duties with stations such as KPIX-TV, KCBS, KQED, among many others. Currently carrying out sports and traffic reporting duties for Bloomberg 960, Brian Drake spends time between reports and carefully guarded morning and evening hours cranking out action/adventure tales.

Brian Drake lives in California with his wife and two cats, and when he's not writing he is usually blasting along the back roads in his Corvette with his wife telling him not to drive so fast, but the engine is so loud he usually can't hear her.

You will find him regularly blogging at:
www.briandrake88.blogspot.com

Made in the USA
Las Vegas, NV
16 January 2021